ENTERTAINING & EDUCATING YOUR PRESCHOOL CHILD

Robyn Gee and Susan Meredith

Designed by Kim Blundell

Illustrated by Sue Stitt, Kim Blundell and Jan Nesbitt

Special Consultants: Dr. Peter Hope, Consultant Paediatrician, John Radcliffe Hospital, Oxford, Hank Williams, play development consultant, Ginny Laight, Lesley Lees and Carol Cook

Part 1 – Birth to 2½ years

Contents of Part 1

In the first part of this book you will find plenty of ideas to help you entertain babies, from birth through toddlerhood and up to the age of 2½. (The second part of the book contains similar but more advanced ideas suitable for the 2½-5 age group.) None of the activities requires a great deal of preparation or special equipment. The time you have for playing will be limited and, in any case, children in this age group appreciate variety of entertainment most of all.

It is now known that babies and toddlers are capable of much more than was thought hitherto and that in fact children learn more and at greater speed during their pre-school years than at any other time in their lives. Even the very youngest babies are ready to start learning about the world around them and can become bored unless someone provides them with the stimulation that they cannot seek out for themselves. The first few pages of the book in particular concentrate on ways of entertaining babies in the first few months of life.

It is not always immediately obvious how certain activities can help a baby to learn. The introduction to each of the topics in the book includes a brief outline of the activities' learning value. Quite often their greatest value lies in the emotional satisfaction babies get from having a parent's full attention and interest, even for only short periods.

No very precise guidelines have been given on the suitable age for each activity, as babies develop at widely differing rates. However, they do tend to go through certain stages of development in roughly the same order so that while it is hard to say exactly when a stage will be reached, it is easier to predict which stage will be reached next. The chart at the back of this section lists some of the stages of development.

Adults can play a very important role in helping a baby or toddler to practise new skills and to learn to play constructively by giving help and encouragement, and by providing the necessary materials. It is worth bearing in mind, however, that even babies need freedom to explore their environment in their own way and that they will develop basic skills without your having to provide constant stimulation. Whatever you do, you cannot make babies reach a certain stage of development sooner than their bodies and brains will allow.

It is important that parents recognize their own needs as well as their child's and do not feel obliged to provide activities that they would not enjoy themselves. Babies and toddlers are very sensitive to mood and can be confused and hurt by a contradiction between a parent's actions and attitude. For a joint activity to be successful, it has to be enjoyable for both of you.

THINGS TO LOOK AT

Having things to look at provides very young babies with one of their chief sources of stimulation, especially when they are still too young to be able to hold things.

People used to think that newborn babies could not see at all but it is now known that they are simply long-sighted and can only see clearly things that are about 25cm (10in) from their nose. They respond to very bright colours, though everything looks rather two-dimensional to them at first. By the time they are six months old, their eyesight is almost as good as adults'.

Giving babies plenty of things to look at not only helps to keep them entertained but also helps them begin to learn to recognize objects and people, and improves their eyesight by exercising and strengthening the muscles used for focusing.

Faces

The distance babies can see at birth happens to be the approximate distance from the crook of a person's arm to their face. Research has shown that babies are more interested in looking at the human face than any other object.

By looking at a baby as you hold him, and smiling and talking, you give him practice in focusing, help him to get to know the human face and you encourage him to return the smiles and so take one of the first steps in communicating with people.

First toys

Apart from faces, young babies have a definite preference for certain other types of objects to look at. These do not need to be real toys as everything is new to them and potentially interesting.

Always give the baby plenty of time to respond to the things you show him. Babies have much slower reactions than adults. You can try tucking objects down the side of his cot or pram mattress.* Don't worry, this will not make him squint.

Babies like things that:

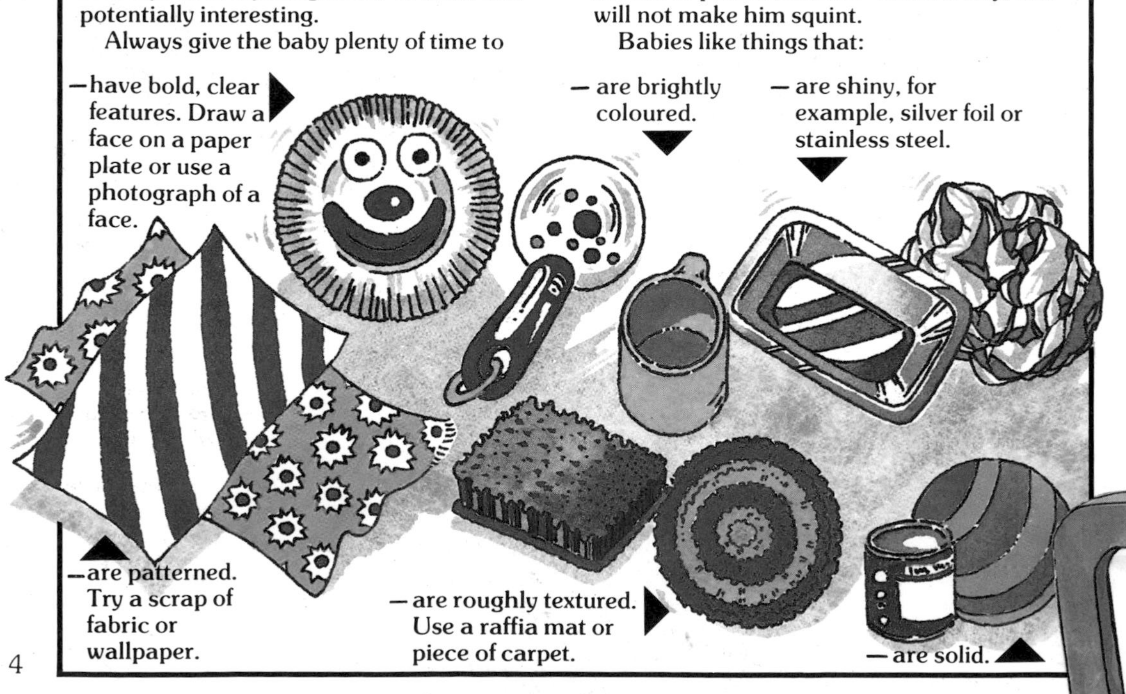

– have bold, clear features. Draw a face on a paper plate or use a photograph of a face.

– are brightly coloured.

– are shiny, for example, silver foil or stainless steel.

– are patterned. Try a scrap of fabric or wallpaper.

– are roughly textured. Use a raffia mat or piece of carpet.

– are solid.

Babies start swiping at things at about three months old so beware of anything that could be harmful if it were grabbed or fell down. See page 12 for more about safety.

Mobiles

Once a baby's head stops flopping over to one side when she is lying on her back, you can start hanging objects above her cot, pram or changing mat, or you can hang them near her chair. It is useful to have ideas for making your own mobiles so you can provide variety.

For a very simple mobile, just hang a single, lightweight object, such as a balloon, on a piece of thread from a drawing pin in the ceiling. The lighter the mobile, the more it will move in a draught and so catch the baby's attention.

For a more elaborate mobile, try fixing a hook in the ceiling, hanging a coat-hanger from it on a piece of string and tying a number of objects to the hanger with thread. It may take you a while to get the objects to balance. Try to arrange them so as to emphasize the differences in their size, shape, colour and texture, and replace or rearrange them regularly to prevent boredom. Here are a few ideas for things to use:

Card or fabric cut or folded into interesting shapes and decorated with felt pen, gummed shapes, glitter or sequins.
Silver foil, slightly crumpled up and/or with holes made in it.
Christmas decorations
Balloons
Foil bottle tops
Yoghurt pots
Ribbons

Cot-hangers

A good way of giving a young baby things to look at in her cot is to attach them to a length of string or elastic stretched tightly across the cot and fastened securely to the bars at either side. You can either thread bulldog clips on to the string and clip the objects up or tie them on. If you use elastic for this, they will bounce if they are touched.

You can use almost any lightweight object, including the ones suggested above for mobiles.* Again, emphasize the contrast between the objects and change them often.

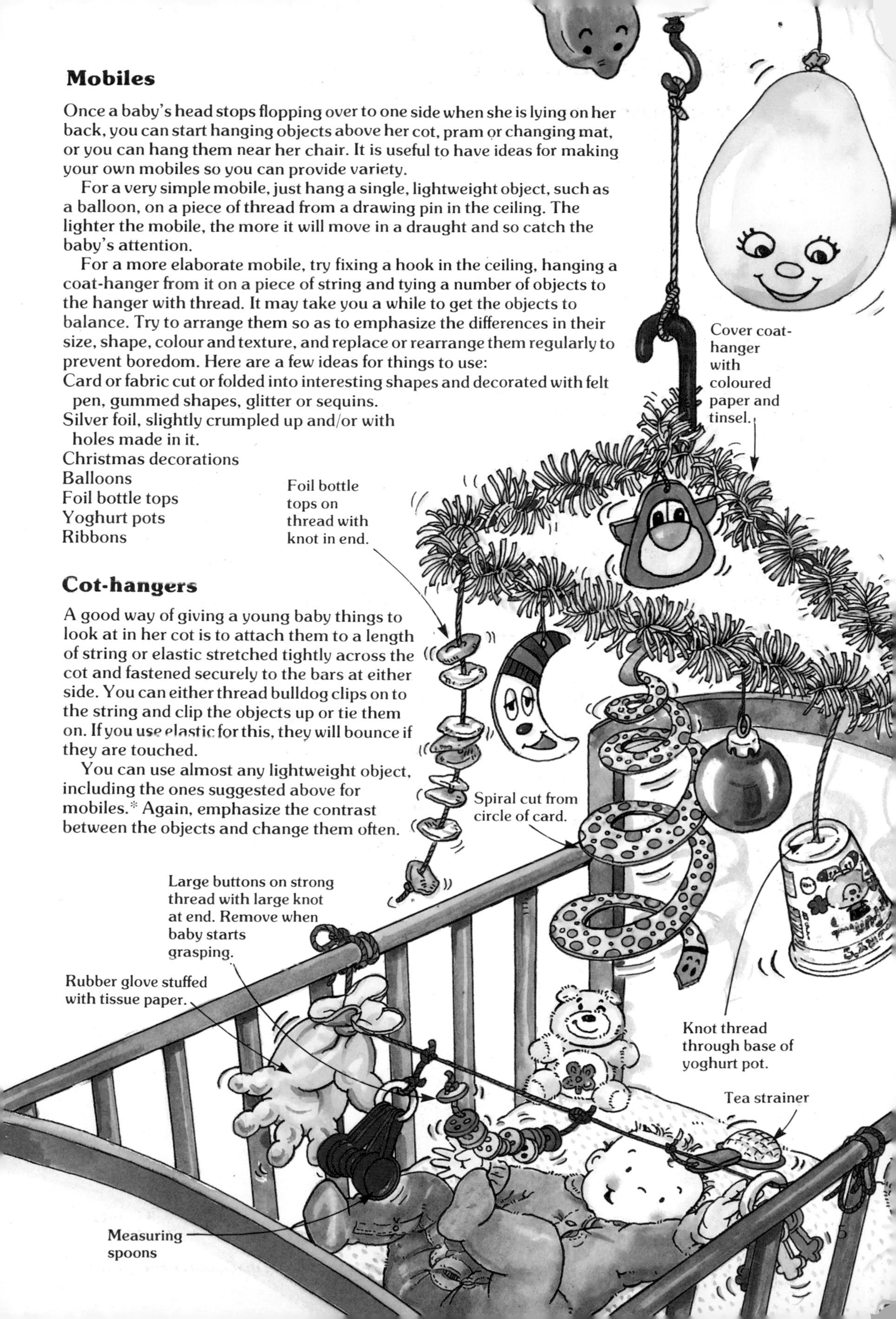

Providing variety

This is essential for young babies because their attention span is extremely short. Besides having a variety of things to look at, they need to spend time in different places and positions.

Spells in a cot or pram can be alternated with periods on a mat or soft rug on the floor, in a baby chair or, from about six weeks old, propped up securely by cushions or pillows in a pram, the corner of an armchair or the middle of a bed.* Try to position the baby so she can look at a room from various angles and take her from room to room with you so she can watch what you are doing. Many babies are happier if there are other people around and activity going on. Many like being carried upright so they can see things from high up, over your shoulder. Lamps, mirrors and the television are often favourite objects to look at.

Peekaboo

Babies love the surprise of seeing someone's face suddenly appear from behind their hands and the accompanying "boo". They begin to learn from this that things continue to exist even when they cannot see them. The game is an excellent way of communicating with a young baby. Vary it by peeping out from behind the furniture. As he gets older, the baby will start to take the initiative at "peekaboo".

Pop-up toys

These provide some of the same pleasures and functions as "peekaboo". Try drawing a face on a wooden spoon and popping it up and down inside an empty kitchen roll tube. You could stick on some wool or cotton wool for hair and brighten up the tube by sticking coloured paper or fabric round it.

Things that move

Babies are fascinated by things that move and may attempt to track something dangling in their field of vision almost from birth. Try dangling a brightly coloured object about 25cm (10in) from the baby's face, at first moving it slowly from side to side, later in other directions.

Older babies enjoy watching the movement of bubbles, balloons and balls, especially if you use these to topple bricks or skittles.

Going out

Taking a baby out in a pram gives her a whole new range of stimulating things to look at. Even at a very early age she will probably enjoy looking at the goods hanging up in the shops and at the people you meet.

If you put her in the garden in her pram, try to position it so she can watch the movement of leaves, washing, shadows or clouds.

THINGS TO LISTEN TO

Babies can hear quite well right from birth, although they may not appear to, and their attention span for listening is even shorter than for looking. They can hear high-pitched sounds better than low-pitched ones at first.

One of the best uses of sound for young babies is to soothe and relax. Gentle talking and music are good for this, and you can buy "soothing sounds" tapes.

Providing sounds for babies to listen to helps them learn to tell where sounds are coming from, which they cannot do at first. As early as four weeks, some babies start turning towards sounds they hear.

Voices

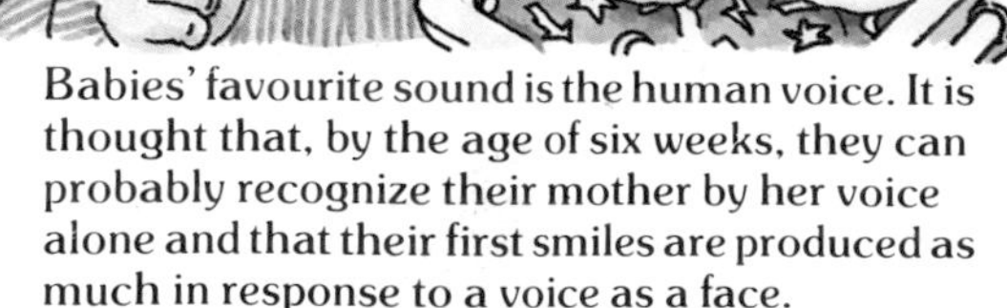

Babies' favourite sound is the human voice. It is thought that, by the age of six weeks, they can probably recognize their mother by her voice alone and that their first smiles are produced as much in response to a voice as a face.

Besides calming and reassuring them, talking to babies right from birth lays the foundation for their own ability to talk later. They enjoy "baby talk" because they like rhythm, rhyme and repetition, but don't worry if you find that difficult to do, as they need to hear proper talk, too. A young baby may be happy to listen to you talking to someone else for a while, even on the telephone. It is also worth singing songs, reciting nursery rhymes and playing records or cassettes of these from birth. For more about talking to babies, see pages 14-17.

Rattles and other sounds

Besides choosing from the many sound-producing toys you can buy, it is easy to improvise your own to provide variety. Until a baby can hold things, you obviously have to make them sound for her.

Try putting any of the following into empty containers and sealing the tops firmly.**

Rice
Pasta
Beans
Lentils
Salt
Water
Earth
Sand
Pebbles
Flower seeds
Clothes-pegs
Bottle tops
Paper clips
Buttons
Beads
Marbles

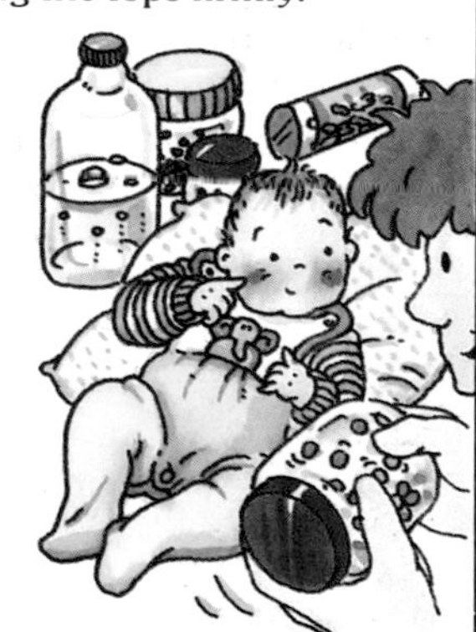

You could also buy a little bell from a pet shop, sew it to ribbon or elastic and add it to a mobile or cot-hanger, or even fasten it round the baby's wrist for short periods. Once the baby starts grasping, move it out of reach. She could choke on it.

Make a point of letting the baby listen to any of the ordinary household objects you are using, for example, keys being jangled, paper crumpled or drinks stirred.

Loud noises

Babies tend to be frightened by sudden loud noises, such as a doorbell ringing, or even a cough or a laugh. Very high or low-pitched noises can also scare them.

On the other hand, more continuous loud noises made, for example, by a washing machine, vacuum cleaner or running tap may fascinate and quieten a fretful baby.

Telling where sounds come from

You can give a baby useful practice in locating sounds by speaking or making a noise at different points in the room, starting close to him. Always show him afterwards what made each sound so he comes to associate it with its source.

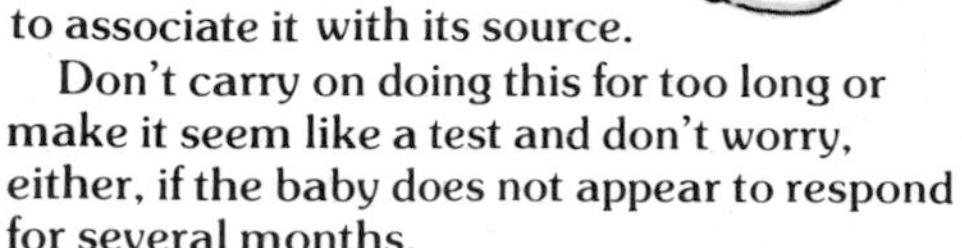

Don't carry on doing this for too long or make it seem like a test and don't worry, either, if the baby does not appear to respond for several months.

Never leave a baby alone when she is propped up like this.
***See page 12 for a safety note about these once a baby can hold things.*

THINGS TO FEEL AND HOLD

Babies start learning about the world through their sense of touch right from birth, although they cannot hold things until they are about three months old. Picking up different objects, handling them and putting them down again is a complex skill that babies spend much of their first year trying to master, as their muscles strengthen and their eyesight and co-ordination between their eyes and hands improve. The way newborn babies try to grasp objects put into the palm of their hand is not deliberate, but is an involuntary reflex action.

The best thing you can do to ensure that a baby's manipulative skills develop to the full is simply to provide as wide a variety of different, safe objects as possible for practising on. Babies may not appear to do very much with the objects but they are learning all the time not only what they feel like but how they behave when treated in a certain way. This is necessary before they can begin to use objects successfully as tools.

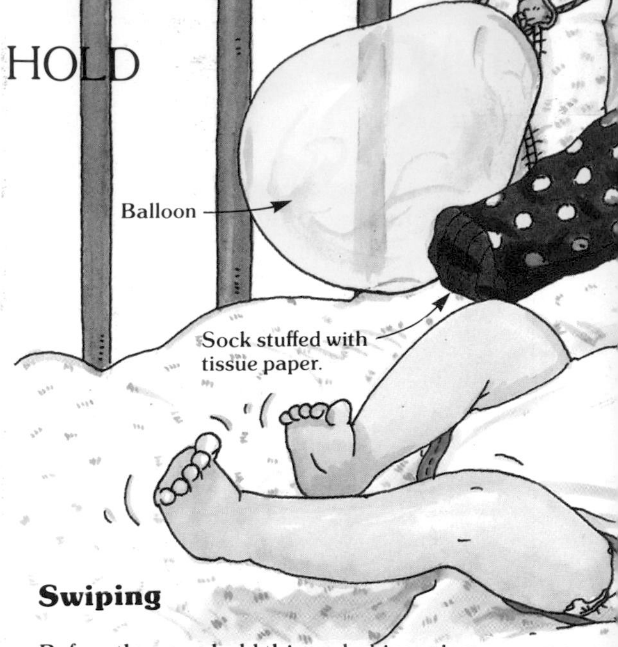

Swiping

Before they can hold things, babies enjoy swiping. Try attaching some foil, a balloon and a sock stuffed with tissue paper to elastic and adding them to the baby's cot-hanger (see page 5) so that they are within arm's reach. At first he will hit the objects by chance but, as he notices them moving, he will gradually realize that there is a connection between what he is seeing and what his hands are doing, and he will start to reach out deliberately.

People

Above all else, most babies like the sensation of being held and cuddled. It is thought that the grasp reflex babies are born with may date from prehistoric times, when they clung to their mothers' fur for safety. In many parts of the world it is still the norm for mothers to carry their babies constantly. The most practical way of doing this is to use a sling. Even the most fretful babies are often soothed and comforted by the closeness, warmth, movement and possibly heartbeat, which they have been used to in the womb.

Massage

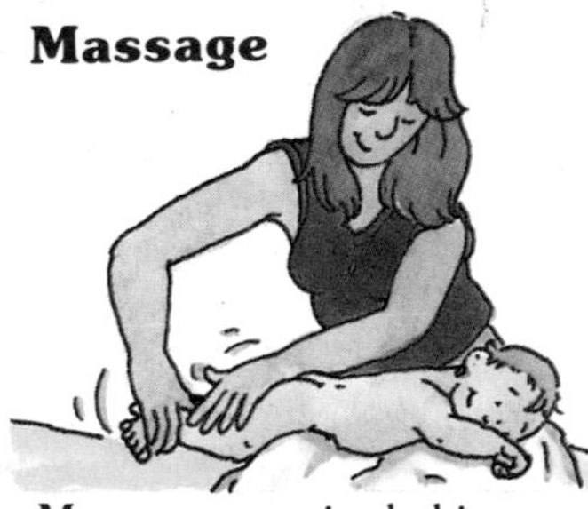

Massage can give babies a feeling of physical and emotional well-being, just as it does older people. It is advisable to learn the technique at a baby massage class, though there are books on the subject. The relaxing effect of massage probably benefits fretful babies most. It is best to massage the baby without his clothes in a very warm room though you can massage through clothes if necessary. You may be able to massage some parts of the body with the baby in your lap or arms.

Things to lie on

As very young babies spend so much time in a cot or pram, it is worth providing them with extra-comfortable bed-clothes, the softer and warmer to the touch, the better. Some people recommend sheepskins. For kicking sessions on the floor, a young baby needs a soft rug or blanket to lie on. As she gets older, let her feel different surfaces such as carpet or grass.

Weather permitting, it is good for babies to spend time with no clothes on so they can get to know the different parts of their body and feel the air against their skin.

If the objects make a noise when he hits them, so much the better. Use rattles, too, or buy bells from a pet shop and add them to the balloon. You can also press tiny bells through the largest hole in an air-flow golf ball (make sure they cannot come out again) and then suspend several of these.

Swiping is important not only for developing hand/eye co-ordination but also because it makes babies feel less passive as they realize their actions can affect the things around them.

Kicking

Babies like feeling with their feet as well as their hands and enjoy kicking against things that move. These need to be quite large as the baby cannot see them. Try suspending crumpled paper, balloons, and inflatable armbands or cushions across the bottom of the cot on strong elastic, and attach bells or rattles to them.

Kicking in a bouncing chair is enjoyable both for the movement itself and for the sense of control it gives a baby when she realizes it is her kicking that causes the movement.

Feel-cloths and comforters

Having different sorts of fabric to feel can provide a baby with a variety of interesting sensations. Try silk, satin, velvet, fur and stretchy materials. He may enjoy having your clothes to hold because they smell of you.

You might like to sew some scraps of different fabric together to make a "feel-cloth". It is often a piece of fabric that a baby adopts as his special "comforter" because of its texture and smell. This is quite normal. Experts refer to comforters as "transitional objects" because they help a baby make the psychological transition from total dependence on the people who look after him to independence.

First attempts at holding

As soon as a baby starts holding his hands open instead of fisted, you can start putting small, light objects into them. He may be able to hold the objects for a few seconds although he will probably not look at what his hands are doing. This is the stage at which rattles are most useful. The sound of the rattle as he waves his arms around prompts him to look at his hands and make the connection between hands, eyes and ears. Give the baby practice at holding in each hand. He will not show a preference for one hand until well past his first birthday.

Taking hold of things

Babies usually start trying to take hold of things at about four months. Watch out for this and put objects alongside the baby in her cot or pram. Until she can grasp them successfully, you could perhaps tie them to the cot bars so they cannot move away when she touches them. At this stage swinging objects across the cot will only frustrate her and a cot gym like the one shown above can be a good buy.

When you hold something out for the baby to take, you need to be patient. You may notice her glancing backwards and forwards between the object and her hand. This is because she has to measure the distance between the two. Give her the chance at least to touch the object before you help by handing it to her.

The best position for a baby to practise picking things up is sitting in a baby chair, preferably one with a tray on which you can put a selection of toys. Don't give her more than two or three to begin with or she will feel confused and, in any case, she needs practice in holding and handling as well as picking up. Replace the objects one by one to stave off boredom.

Once a baby can hold things, safety becomes especially important as she will put everything in her mouth.* Her mouth is more sensitive than her fingers at this stage so she can learn more about the objects by doing this.

Ideas for things to hold

Some babies are not content to hold and examine one object for more than a few seconds at a time and drop things constantly through boredom as well as incompetence. Variety is all-important and you need to have a large supply of safe, household objects always to hand. It is worth keeping a collection of things the baby can play with ready in each room. Below and opposite are some ideas.

Living room

Books. Babies are fascinated by hinges and love opening and shutting books, and turning the pages, besides looking at them.
Old magazines and catalogues
Cotton reels. Try threading them on string or ribbon.
Ribbon*
Elastic
Ball of wool. Make sure the end cannot work loose.*
Blank cassettes
Playing cards
Drinks mats
Cushions*

Bathroom

Baby's personal possessions: sponge, toothbrush, comb, hairbrush, nappies.
Soap dish. With soap inside, this makes a rattle.
Talcum powder tins*
Cream jars*
Plastic bottles*
Toilet roll tube
Clean towel
Nail-brush
Eye-bath
Strip of bandage
Roll of sticking plaster

*See page 12 for notes on safety and hygiene.

Select objects for the differences in their shape, size, weight and texture (rough, smooth, soft, hard, stiff, stretchy, for example). Bear in mind, too, what makes things interesting to look at (see pages 4 and 6) and to listen to (see page 7) so the baby learns to use his different senses together.

Try to develop an eye for anything that is a potential new "toy" such as packaging, an empty container or the lining from a chocolate box. Hide away familiar playthings when they become boring and they may seem fresh and exciting again a few days later.

If you have a number of small objects that would be unsafe to give to the baby individually or that he keeps dropping, you could try threading them on to a shoe-lace or length of string and tying the ends firmly. Or you could tie the objects to curtain rings and sew these securely to a strong piece of plain fabric or a plain cushion.

Kitchen*

Spoons (plastic, metal and wooden)
Empty yoghurt pots and margarine tubs
Unopened packets, tins and strong bags of food
Stainless steel (egg cups, toast rack)
Washed fruit and vegetables
Rubber rings from preserving jars
Plastic containers
Plastic or paper cups and plates
Metal teapot
Metal kettle
Saucepans
Saucepan lids
Egg poaching pan
Cake and bun tins
Trays
Ice-cube tray
Foil dishes
Egg boxes
Tea caddy
Coffee tin
Biscuit tin
Fish slice
Potato masher
Ladle
Spatulas
Sieve
Colander
Tea strainer
Whisk
Funnel
Pastry brush
Paper cake cases
Doilies
Drinking straws
Kitchen roll tube
Rubber gloves
New dish-cloth
Clean tea towel
Napkin rings
Table mats

Miscellaneous

Plastic bottles. To make a bubble bottle, fill a transparent, screw-topped bottle with water and a squirt of washing-up liquid, or, for a slightly different sort of bubble, use a tablespoon of cooking oil. You could add food colouring too.
Rattles, home-made as well as bought. See page 7 for ideas.
Clean, empty boxes, jars, tins and bottles (not glass) with or without lids. Hinged lids are the most fun.
Balls of different sizes (ping-pong, tennis, football)
Paper of all sorts, except newspaper, for crumpling, tearing, rustling, hiding behind.
Parcels. Wrap a favourite toy loosely in one or two thicknesses of paper without sticking it down. Or put it in a paper bag.
Ball of string. Make sure the end cannot work loose.*
Mirrors. Only let him have unbreakable baby mirrors to hold.
Windows and walls. Hold the baby up so he can hit, stroke, wipe and scratch.
Balloons, not fully blown up.
Pieces of well sand-papered wood.
Rulers (wooden, plastic and metal)
Roll of adhesive tape
Polystyrene packing
Wickerwork baskets and bowls
New flowerpots and saucers
New dustpan and brush
Scraps of fabric
Clothes-pegs
Large pebbles
Bunch of keys

Getting more skilled

As the baby's manipulative skills improve, you can help in a variety of ways.

★ Offer him objects at different angles so he has to work out how best to take them.

★ Give him larger or heavier things that he has to get both hands to.

★ Give him things with holes to poke his fingers into (air-flow ball, draining spoon) or put his hands and feet through (bangle, roll of adhesive tape, wrist band).

★ Hand him a second object and he will gradually learn not to drop the first but to hold an object in each hand and, eventually, to hold two things in one hand.

Food

Meal times are a good opportunity to practise manipulative skills. Finger feeding and holding a cup are two of the first things a baby can do for herself. She can also practise holding a spoon well before she can feed herself efficiently with it.

Making a mess with food can be seen as the very earliest form of creative play. It is also thought that being allowed to do this helps to avoid faddy eating habits.

The pincer grip

By about nine months, most babies are developing the ability to hold things between finger and thumb, pincer-like, rather than in their palm only. To master the pincer grip they need practice with very small, fine objects. For safety's sake, things to eat are the best. Try small pieces of potato and carrot, peas, bread, biscuits and hundreds-and-thousands. The baby will also be fascinated by lengths of wool, thread or string.*

Safety and hygiene

Once a baby starts reaching out for things, it is vitally important to be aware of the possible dangers of any object he might get hold of. If you are in doubt about something, don't leave it lying around.

★ Babies put everything in their mouths. Never let a baby have anything small enough to swallow or choke on, or put in his nose or ears. This includes larger objects from which small parts could get detached when tugged or chewed. The safest containers are ones with screw tops. Babies cannot usually unscrew these until they are about 18 months old but they can lift press-on tops earlier.

Don't give a baby objects painted with paint that may contain lead, avoid newsprint and wash out empty bottles very thoroughly. Avoid completely bottles that have had bleach or cleaning fluids in them.

★ Don't let him have anything that could suffocate him. This includes plastic bags, and cushions or pillows if there is any chance he might fall on top of them.

★ Beware of anything that could strangle him or get wound round his fingers or toes and cut off the blood supply. Don't leave him playing alone with things like ribbon.

★ Avoid pointed objects that he could dig in his skin, put down his throat or poke in his eyes, ears or nose, and objects with sharp edges that he could cut himself on. Throw away yoghurt pots when they crack.

★ Avoid objects heavy enough to hurt if he dropped them on himself.

★ Make sure all his playthings are clean. Objects that have been in contact with food are the main danger and it is safest to sterilize cooking utensils before giving them to a baby under nine months. Just wash other things regularly in washing-up liquid or baking soda, rinse and drip dry.

**See "safety" above.*

Learning to let go

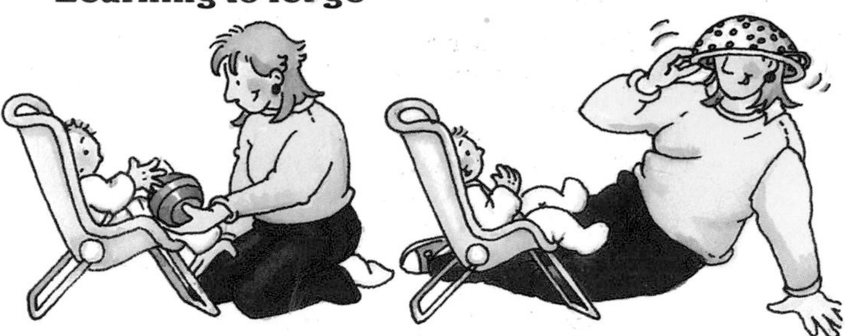

Most babies cannot let go of things deliberately until they are about ten months old. The best way to help a baby do this is to put your open hand beneath something she is holding so she can feel it resting on a flat surface.

Once she has got the idea, you can start playing games of "give and take". Encourage her to let go by asking her to give you what she is holding and by doing something amusing with it before you give it back again.

Playing ball

Once a baby can let go of things, she may be ready for an elementary game of ball. To begin with, sit her on the floor with her legs apart and gently throw a ball so that it lands between them. She will probably try to pat it, if not throw it back to you.

You can also throw the ball gently into her lap as she sits in her chair. She will be delighted to have "caught" it and will push it off again for you to retrieve.

Dropping things

This becomes a favourite pastime when a baby realizes she can let go. Babies do not drop things to annoy but because they are practising a new skill, are curious to discover what happens to the things they drop and enjoy the social, turn-taking aspect of the game as you hand things back to them.

When you get fed up with picking things up, you could attach a favourite toy to one end of a length of string, tie the other end to the high chair or pram and try showing the baby how to haul it up again when she has dropped it.*

Alternatively, provide a number of things all at once for her to drop. Include light objects such as paper or balloons as well as heavier ones, things that roll (plastic bottles), bounce (balls) and stay still (cushions, bean bags). To encourage her to aim, try giving her a largish container to drop the things into. A metal tray in the bottom of the container makes an interesting sound.

Emptying and filling

This usually becomes a major preoccupation around a baby's first birthday. Provide containers of different sizes and plenty of suitable-sized objects to empty out of them and put back in again, such as bricks, carrots, clothes-pegs, socks, disposable nappies or playing cards.

The baby will also enjoy unpacking shopping and emptying cupboards. It is worth re-organizing at least one cupboard of household things, perhaps in the kitchen, so he can be allowed to empty it while you work. He may also be intrigued by draw-string bags that he can just get his hand inside.

LEARNING TO TALK

Learning to talk is one of the key developments of a child's first three years and is vital to normal social, emotional and intellectual development.

The rate at which individual children learn to talk varies widely, as does that of all other aspects of development. It depends on temperament and the physical development of the parts of the body used for speech as well as on intellectual ability and stimulation from the environment. It is worth remembering that early progress has no particular bearing on later ability.

Babies start learning language long before they can say any words. Newborn babies prefer the sound of the human voice to any other and talking to them right from birth can play a valuable part in their language development. It not only helps them to learn the rhythms, patterns and intonations of speech but also conveys the idea that talking is a pleasant social activity, which makes them want to participate. To reinforce this idea, it is important to spend some time talking directly to the baby and looking at her while you talk so she feels she has your individual attention. This will also help her to learn the facial expressions that accompany speech.

The suggestions on the following pages may give you some useful starting points for talking to a baby, especially if you feel awkward about talking to someone who cannot reply with words. Babies do respond with a great variety of sounds, however, and listening carefully to these may encourage you to talk back. The charts on pages 42-47 will give you an idea of some of the stages in babies' speech development.

Don't force yourself to oversimplify what you are saying or to use baby talk if this does not come naturally to you. Don't worry either about constantly repeating yourself. Repetition plays an important part in language learning and babies seem to enjoy it.

Things to talk about

When you are doing something for the baby, such as dressing or bathing him, try talking to him about what you are doing. Ask him questions even though you have to supply the answers for him. Show him things and describe them to him, explaining what they are for. When he is old enough to sit in a chair and watch you, you can even give him running commentaries on what you are doing.

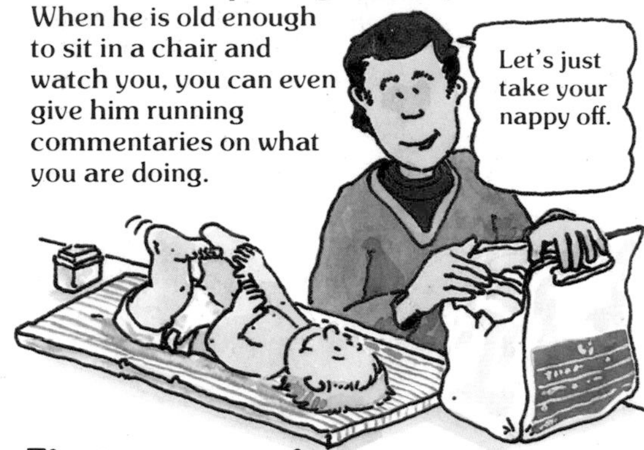

First conversations

Babies need to absorb the patterns of talk as well as individual sounds. If they hear plenty of talking, they soon learn that people speak in turn, with pauses in between. Once a baby has started making deliberate sounds, you can give him practice in making "conversation" by saying something, pausing and waiting for him to respond. When he responds, you reply.

Toys

Certain toys are especially useful for encouraging talking. From about six months, most babies enjoy looking in mirrors. These encourage them to be aware of their mouths and so make sounds.

An unbreakable mirror in a coloured plastic surround is a good buy.

Rhymes and songs

Learning the rhythms of speech is an important part of learning to talk and nursery rhymes often mimic and emphasize these rhythms. Repetition of the same words over and over again helps babies to recognize particular sounds and eventually to realize that certain sounds have certain meanings. Rhymes and songs with actions to go with them give extra clues as to meaning. (See pages 39-41.)

Pat-a-cake
Pat-a-cake
Baker's man . . .

Books

It is worth looking at books even with a very young baby. Talk about the pictures just as you would with an older child. A simple picture always accompanied by the same word or words is a great aid to realizing that words have meaning. Later, books provide opportunities to learn new words. Read simple stories, too. Eventually the child will start joining in. (See pages 18-20 for more about books.)

Starting to understand

Babies have to understand quite a lot of language before they can say anything themselves. They learn the meaning of a word by hearing it used repeatedly in different sentences but always associated with the same thing. Saying a single word over and over again in an attempt to make a baby understand it or to imitate the sound before she understands its meaning is not very useful.

From about eight months onwards, when a baby is starting to understand a few sounds and words, it is worth taking a bit of trouble to help her understanding develop.

★ Stress the key words in your sentences and try not to replace them with pronouns.

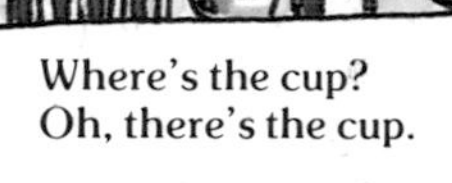

★ Use the baby's name instead of "you" or "your".

Here's a biscuit for Emily.

Here's a biscuit for Mummy.

★ Exaggerate your intonation and facial expressions, and match your words with actions.

. . . high up in the air.

★ Talk about things the baby is looking at and about things that interest her such as toys or food.

. . . a red brick and a blue brick.

From about 12 months, toy telephones are helpful and making soft toys and puppets speak can also encourage conversation.

To make a finger puppet, cut out a semicircle of card or felt, curl it into a tube shape and stick it so it fits your finger. Draw or stick on the features.

Two telephones linked by plastic tubing allow you to talk from room to room.

First words

Most babies use their first real words (that is, sounds with specific meanings attached to them) round about their first birthday. First words are often surprisingly difficult to identify, as it is hard to sort out the accidental from the intentional. They are nearly always labels – names for people, animals and things that are important to them, though social words such as "bye-bye", "no" and "thank you" are often among the first as well. You may find that some words have a very general meaning. Many babies start off by using the same word for any type of food or drink.

Some babies learn lots of words as soon as they begin to speak but it is more usual to learn between one and three a month for the first few months. Some words may only be used for a few days or weeks and then disappear from their vocabulary for quite a time. If a baby is concentrating hard on learning to walk, progress with talking may slow down temporarily.

At around 18 months, toddlers often start to learn new words much more rapidly and by the time they are two may know as many as 200 words. During this period they also learn to use more varied intonation to indicate whether a word is a label, a greeting, a demand or a question.

★ The more effort you make to understand the baby's first attempts at words, the harder she will try to say more.

★ Babies often invent words. Don't correct these or pretend not to understand or the baby will be confused and discouraged. They will be replaced by the proper words eventually.

★ The pronunciation of words is often simplified. Babies often leave consonants off the beginning or end of words and some children have difficulty with certain consonants until they are about five. Don't try to make a child pronounce words correctly, though you could give the right version in your reply.

★ Help the baby to use the words she knows whenever possible and use them in your own conversation.

Putting words together

Shortly before their second birthday, children often start putting two words together to make their meaning clearer; soon after it they may begin to form simple sentences. From now on their range of vocabulary and ability to combine words, use grammar and take part in dialogue steadily improve, provided they get enough encouragement and stimulation.

Gradually they realize that words can be used to describe actions (verbs), where things are (prepositions), who owns what (possessives) and what things are like (adjectives). You may notice a child introducing a different part of speech or aspect of grammar (such as the past tense or plurals) and practising it intensively before moving on to something else.

★ Make language as interesting as possible by making time to have conversations and taking questions seriously and trying to answer them.

Games to play

These are good for developing understanding, encouraging first words and extending vocabulary. The conversation involved and the repetition of words in context are particularly helpful.

Asking games. Once a baby understands a few words and starts "asking" for things with sounds or gestures, you can turn asking into a game. Sit opposite the baby on the floor, put a ball or other toy in front of him, then hold out your hands and ask him to pass it to you. If he does, roll it back, then ask him to pass it again. Once he gets the idea, wait for him to "ask" before rolling it back.

Fetching games. With a mobile baby, you can extend asking games to become fetching games. Choose an object the baby can see and that he knows the name for and ask him to fetch it for you. Pointing helps in this game but, up to about twelve months, babies tend to look at the pointing finger rather than what it is pointing at.

Once the baby can fetch things that are visible, you can ask him to fetch things that are out of sight but are always kept in the same place. Later, he will be able to look for things that are not kept anywhere in particular.

Hiding and finding games. Start these very simply, as it takes babies a long time to realize that things are still there even when they cannot see them. At first, let the baby see where you are hiding something and always hide it in the same place, perhaps leaving a bit showing. Once he has got the idea, change the hiding place but still let him see where it is. Eventually this will develop into "hunt-the-thimble" with you taking it in turns to hide things.

Copying games. Babies and toddlers learn a tremendous amount by copying people. Try sitting in front of a big mirror together. Point to the different parts of your body and encourage the baby to copy you, while you name the parts. Later you can play copying games with actions such as jumping and bending to help develop understanding and use of verbs.

Toddlers often enjoy making happy, sad or cross faces in front of a mirror and this helps them learn to understand that faces can express how people feel.

★ Don't restrict your own vocabulary too much. Toddlers understand much more than they can express and learn words by hearing them in context.

★ Don't make a child correct mistakes of grammar. She will only be put off talking. She will learn good grammar by hearing it spoken around her.

I gived you a letter.

Yes, you gave me a letter.

★ Don't interrupt or finish the sentence if a child is struggling for words. The process of talking actually helps children to form new concepts.

BOOKS, PICTURES AND STORIES

It is never too early to start showing a baby books. Look at them together as soon as you can balance both the baby and the book on your knee.

To begin with, small babies get as much enjoyment from the movement of the pages turning, the noise of the paper and the sound of your voice, as you talk or read, as they do from the pictures, which they see as colours, shapes and patterns.

Gradually the shapes become familiar and recognizable and they start to associate specific sounds with each shape. Then they learn to turn the pages by themselves, to point to things they recognize, to name things and eventually to listen to and join in stories.

The best reason for introducing babies to books is that they enjoy them. Many parents find that books are the single most effective way of keeping their baby happily entertained. But babies and toddlers can also learn a great deal from looking at books.

Books help to develop their visual understanding and ability to notice detail. They are also very valuable in the development of language skills, helping them learn to listen, understand and speak and encouraging a desire to communicate. They broaden their horizons by stimulating the imagination, helping them to make sense of situations they have experienced and introducing them to new ones, and by showing them how other people feel and behave.

Later on, books will have a vital role to play in a child's more formal education. Early enjoyment of them will help to form a good groundwork for this.

It is worth remembering, even with this very young age group, that there is no point in trying to force books on a child who would clearly prefer to be doing something else. There is always the risk that you may put him off books.

Choosing books

First picture books. To start with, choose a few books that have clear, simple, colourful illustrations of objects or animals that are part of a baby's everyday world. There should be only one or two illustrations per page and no confusing detail. From as early as three months, the baby will be able to focus briefly on the pictures. Include in this early collection one or two board and bath books which will stand up to handling and chewing.

From about 12 months, as the baby acquires more words, he will gradually be able to cope with more and more complicated pictures.

Catalogues. These are often very popular with babies, who particularly enjoy seeing things like other babies and familiar toys, clothes and furniture. They also enjoy tearing the paper. Colourful magazines and photograph albums can also be good entertainment.

Pop-up books. Pop-ups, books with flaps to lift and tags to pull, "feely" books, squeaky books, cloth, board and bath books are all good for getting babies interested and involved in books. They need to be tough if they are to last long.

Nursery rhyme and action rhyme books. These are invaluable for reminding you of old favourites and perhaps introducing you to new ones. They usually remain popular for a long time so choose a good sturdy edition with detailed illustrations.

First story books. Talking about pictures in books will lead on naturally to reading stories. You will probably be able to start introducing some very simple stories from about 15 months onwards. Some toddlers find it impossible to sit still and listen, however, while others will listen to stories they do not even understand, enjoying the sound and rhythm of the words.

Choose stories with few words and plenty of pictures which do a lot of the story-telling work. The words will only gradually become as important as the pictures. Stories which repeat catchy, rhythmical phrases over and over again give toddlers something to listen for and enjoy even when they cannot really follow the story-line. Many traditional folk tales do this.

Try out as wide a variety of different stories as you can to see what the child prefers. Borrowing books from a library allows you to do this at no expense.

Stories involving familiar, everyday routines are usually popular with small children. They like to explore how like or unlike other people they are. They may also enjoy fantasy stories. It is worth watching out for, and taking seriously, any sign of a child being disturbed or frightened by a story.

Information books. It is useful for a child to realize that books are a source of factual information as well as stories. Once he starts to outgrow his first simple picture books, replace them with some information books. Zoos, farms and vehicles are popular subjects. He may also enjoy the pictures in nature books aimed at older children.

Books are also helpful for learning about things like colours, shapes and sizes and, by the age of two-and-a-half, it is worth having alphabet and numbers books too.

Making your own books

This is a good cheap way of providing babies with plenty of variety in their library. Punch holes in pieces of card and thread them together with string, wool or ribbon to make a simple book.

A small scrap book or photograph album also makes a good baby book. The kind of album that has a single plastic pocket per page is ideal for small babies.

Select pictures of things you know the baby particularly enjoys looking at to put in the book. Include your own photographs and drawings of familiar objects.

You could make a "first words" book for the baby. As soon as he can say a word, stick a picture of it in the book. This will also act as a record for you. Write the word beneath the picture so he can gradually absorb the idea that words are written down as well as spoken.

Old Christmas, birthday and postcards can also be made into books. Cut the backs off, make holes down one side and thread them together.

Looking at books together

The best way of encouraging a baby to like books is to look at them together, as often as the baby wants to and you can find the time. She will enjoy the physical closeness and the feeling of shared experience, and this can help to strengthen the emotional links between you.

You can gradually introduce special times of day for looking at books together. They can help to quieten a toddler down before a nap or bedtime and also provide a useful means of resting without sleeping. Books can also be a great help in passing the time on journeys or whenever you have to sit and wait for something.

Looking at books alone

It is worth encouraging a baby from the beginning to look at books by herself. This starts with simply playing with board, bath or cloth books but once she can turn the pages she may be happy to spend short periods looking at the pictures by herself. This is more likely to happen if she is used to seeing the people around her looking at books.

It is important that her books are kept where she can reach them easily, perhaps in a decorated box in a cosy reading corner.

Telling stories

It is a good idea to accustom children to listening to stories that are not written in books. These can help to develop the imagination and it is useful to learn the skill of listening and understanding without a visual aid.

Most toddlers love hearing stories about themselves and the people close to them. These help them to develop a sense of identity, to use their memories and to picture the past. Photographs can provide a helpful starting point for telling family stories.

Tapes

Many toddlers enjoy listening to tapes, especially those you have compiled yourself. They are useful for times when you cannot give a child your full attention, such as on car journeys, and for encouraging resting and going to sleep. Keep any stories very short and intersperse them with rhymes and songs.

Television

At first, babies see television pictures as changing colours and patterns but they slowly begin to make sense of the jumble of images and sounds and some time during their second year will probably start to watch some programmes with interest.

Television has a lot to contribute to a child's understanding and imaginative development. Stories can be brought alive by movement and sound effects, and programmes which suggest things to do are valuable.

A toddler has a very short attention span, however. When she loses interest, turn the television off; if it is kept on as constant background entertainment, it will be hard for her to concentrate fully on other things, and play and books will have to compete with the television for her attention. Whenever you can, watch programmes with a toddler, so you can talk about and help to explain them.

ENERGETIC PLAY

Babies gain control of their bodies very gradually, starting from the top and moving downwards, so they learn to hold their heads up before they sit, sit before they crawl and usually crawl before they walk. The rate at which different babies go through these stages varies widely and depends on personality as well as physical development. Like older people, babies differ in how active they are.

Once a baby is mobile, provided you take basic safety precautions (see page 25), it is better on the whole to encourage adventurousness than to overprotect. A liking for energetic play is good for increasing strength and agility, improving co-ordination and balance, developing self-confidence and sociability, and for all-round general health.

Finding enough space for energetic play can be a problem. Mother-and-toddler groups usually have more space than most homes as well as larger pieces of equipment such as climbing frames and ride-on toys. A park may have playground equipment basic enough for toddlers to try under supervision and at least gives them the opportunity to run until they are tired.

Even very young babies can be energetic and need the freedom to kick their legs and wave their arms without being restricted by too many clothes or bed-clothes. (See pages 8-9.)

Games to play

Physical play with another person is one of a baby's best means of communication; it also helps her to differentiate herself from other people, which she cannot do at first; it helps her to feel at ease with her body and is a good way of using up surplus energy before she is fully mobile.

Some babies enjoy these games more than others and physical play should never be forced on a baby who is not showing obvious signs of enjoyment. A baby is less likely to enjoy physical games when she is tired, unwell, hungry or overfull.

Exercises

Doing gentle exercises with a baby can be fun and increase his body awareness and control besides helping to develop muscles. Baby gym classes are held in some areas.

Arm stretch

Let the baby grasp your thumbs. Holding one arm down by his side, slowly raise the other above his head. Change arms.

Crossovers

With the baby either sitting up or lying on his back, open out his arms to his sides, then cross them back over his chest.

Bicycling

Hold the baby's ankles and gently rotate his legs, first in one direction, then the other. Also let him push his feet against your hands.

Wheelbarrow

With the baby's arms out in front of him, hold his hips and slowly raise his lower half. This is good preparation for somersaults later.

Encouraging physical skills

Don't forget that babies vary in how naturally physically active they are. While you can help a baby to practise the skills he is at the stage of acquiring and encourage him by praising his efforts, you cannot hurry him through the stages quicker than his body and brain will allow.

Holding head up

To hold his head up, a baby needs strength in his neck muscles. Put him on his front and see if he tries to raise his head and shoulders when you:

★ give him your thumbs to hold;

★ speak to him with your face just above his head;

★ shake a rattle just above his head.

Don't insist if the baby hates being put on his front.

Rolling

Being able to roll over gives a baby her first real taste of mobility and means she can at last get to toys that are just out of reach. To encourage her to roll from her back to her side, from about six weeks:

★ lie down alongside her, so she has to roll to get closer to you;

★ put a favourite toy out to her side;

★ kneel over her, then suddenly lower your face or a favourite soft toy. She may roll as she squirms to get out of the way. (Make sure she realizes this is only a game.)

Once she can roll, she may enjoy your nudging her with your head to make her roll or pulling her back with your hand whenever she starts to roll.

Sitting

Most babies cannot sit completely unsupported for about eight months but they appreciate sitting in a baby chair or being propped up with pillows or cushions* from about six weeks. A baby chair you can adjust from a reclining into a more and more upright position as the baby's back gets stronger is a good buy. If you prop the baby in her pram, in the corner of an armchair or on a bed**, ensure that there is a straight slope from her neck to the base of her spine. Putting the cushion under the pram mattress helps. Propping the baby in a cardboard box can also be quite successful as the sides give good support.

To encourage a baby to learn to sit alone :

★ gently pull her up into a sitting position by her hands from about three months old. If she is ready for this, she will raise her head and try to pull herself up;

★ holding her under her arms, sit her on your lap or the edge of a table and speak to her. She may try to straighten up to look at you;

★ as her back gets stronger, say from about six months, sit her on the floor surrounded by pillows, cushions, duvets or rolled-up blankets,* perhaps with a folded blanket under her bottom and her back against an armchair;

★ sit her on the floor for a second and catch her as she overbalances;

★ give her toys that do not roll away and things she cannot easily play with lying down such as a spoon and saucepan lid to bang, an activity centre and toys that fix to the high chair tray by a suction pad.

**Don't leave the baby alone like this. She could suffocate if she fell over.*

Crawling

Some experts think that the co-ordination involved in crawling is good for the brain and develops the same parts that are used for later activities such as reading and writing. Some babies never crawl though, or else crawl sideways, crab-like, or shuffle along on their bottoms and this is nothing to worry about.

You do not need to put a baby in a crawling position. He will get there himself when he is ready, either from his front or from sitting.

★ Put a favourite toy a little way in front of the baby or, better still, sit holding it yourself.

★ Tempt him by opening a low cupboard that you would not mind him investigating.

★ Crawl with him. Have "races" and chasing games, and play hide-and-seek round the furniture.

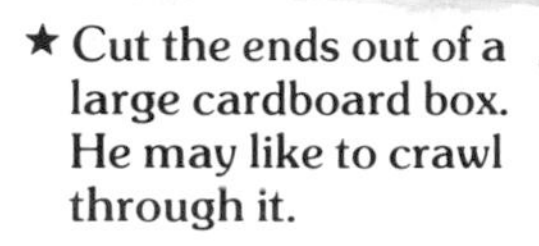

★ Cut the ends out of a large cardboard box. He may like to crawl through it.

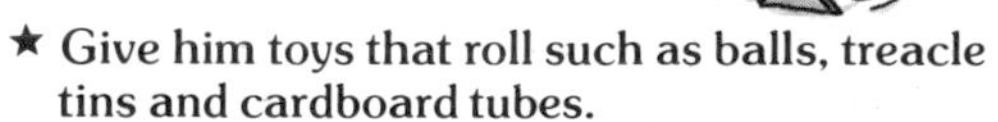

★ Give him toys that roll such as balls, treacle tins and cardboard tubes.

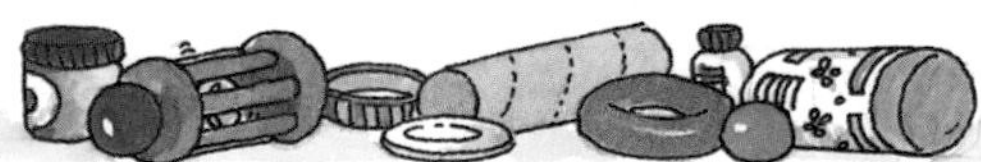

★ Give him toys on wheels. Show him how these roll on their own down a slope. Gradually decrease the slope until it is flat and he may realize he can give the toy a push and then let go.

Once a baby is crawling, let him wear dungarees to protect his knees and don't confine him to a playpen.

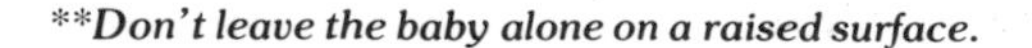

**Don't leave the baby alone on a raised surface.*

Standing

Many babies like to "feel their feet" from an early age.

★ Hold him so he can stand on your lap or any firm surface. At first his legs will buckle, later he will try to bounce.

★ Put him in a bouncer or walker (see page 24).

★ Put a favourite toy on a chair so he has to pull himself up to reach it. A baby learns to stand by pulling himself up on the furniture or people's legs. If you stand him up and then let go, he just collapses. Make sure your furniture can take his weight and that there are no flexes or overhanging tablecloths to pull on.

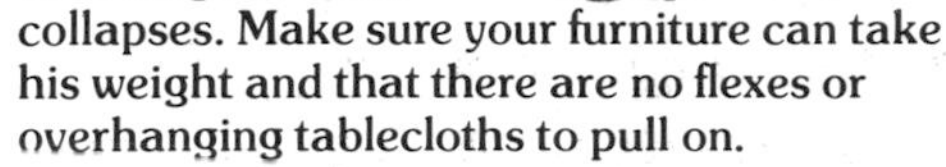

When a baby first learns to stand, he cannot sit down again. Release his hands and lower his bottom gently to the floor.

Climbing

This usually starts with the baby trying to crawl upstairs and climb into armchairs.

★ Show her how to get down by sliding backwards on her tummy. Later you can show her how to come downstairs on her bottom, then how to walk up and down one step at a time, holding on to your hand or the wall.

★ Let her climb up and over you. This way you can save her when she falls.

★ Give her a giant floor cushion to climb on.

★ Give her an old tyre.

★ Stuff an old cardboard box with newspaper.

★ Let her climb on and off ride-on toys.

Walking

Once a baby can stand, she soon starts inching her way along the furniture, holding on, then crosses small gaps (no wider than her arm span) between furniture, then larger gaps which entail leaving go with both hands for a moment. Now she realizes she can stand alone and is almost ready to launch herself into space.

★ Arrange the furniture so she can make her way safely around the room.

★ Walk with her. She will let you know whether she needs to hold both hands, one hand or one finger. Don't leave go to see if she can walk alone. It will shake her confidence and her trust in you.

★ Give her a baby walker: a large push-along toy on wheels. Make sure it will take her weight when she pulls herself up on it. (For another type of walker, see right.)

★ Stand a few paces away and encourage her to walk towards you.

Once she can walk on her own, you can give further encouragement.

★ She will probably enjoy carrying things about. Give her a bag to put things in.

★ Play fetching games (see page 17).

★ Play hide-and-seek around the furniture.

★ Play chasing games. These encourage running and are enjoyed most if there is a second adult to run to.

Toddlers find it quite hard to follow another person or even to walk alongside holding their hand. It is much easier for them to gravitate round a central point. Walking outdoors may be more enjoyable if you take the toddler to a park in a pushchair and let her walk around while you sit down.

Bouncers and walkers

Many parents find these indispensable. Both satisfy babies' desire to be upright, besides strengthening their leg muscles and using up energy. A few babies do not like bouncers so it is worth trying out a friend's before you buy one. Walkers allow a baby to be mobile earlier than he would be otherwise but do not actually teach him how to walk as he does not have to balance himself.

Once a baby can get about under his own steam, interest in bouncers and walkers usually fades quickly. Don't leave a baby in either any longer than he is happy to be there, or for more than an hour in any case. Bouncers especially can be very tiring.

Pull-along toys

These become popular around the time the toddler realizes he can walk backwards and are good for improving balance and co-ordination. The best pull-alongs make a noise and have a low, wide base so they do not keep falling over. You can improvise some of your own.

★ Tie a piece of string to a rattle. Some of the home-made ones suggested on page 7 would work quite well. You could use a heated metal knitting needle to make holes in either end of a plastic container and loop the string through.

★ Thread cotton reels together.

★ Provide a cardboard box with string attached.

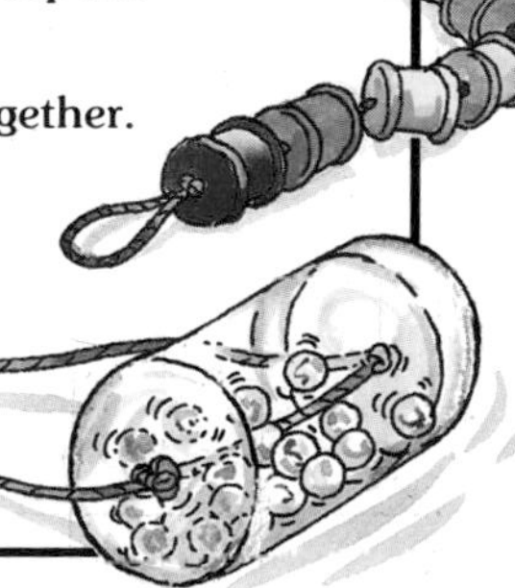

Indoor gym equipment

A plank of wood, about 150cm (5ft) by 30cm (1ft), with the corners rounded down, sandpapered and varnished is very versatile though, for safety's sake, you need to supervise its use closely.

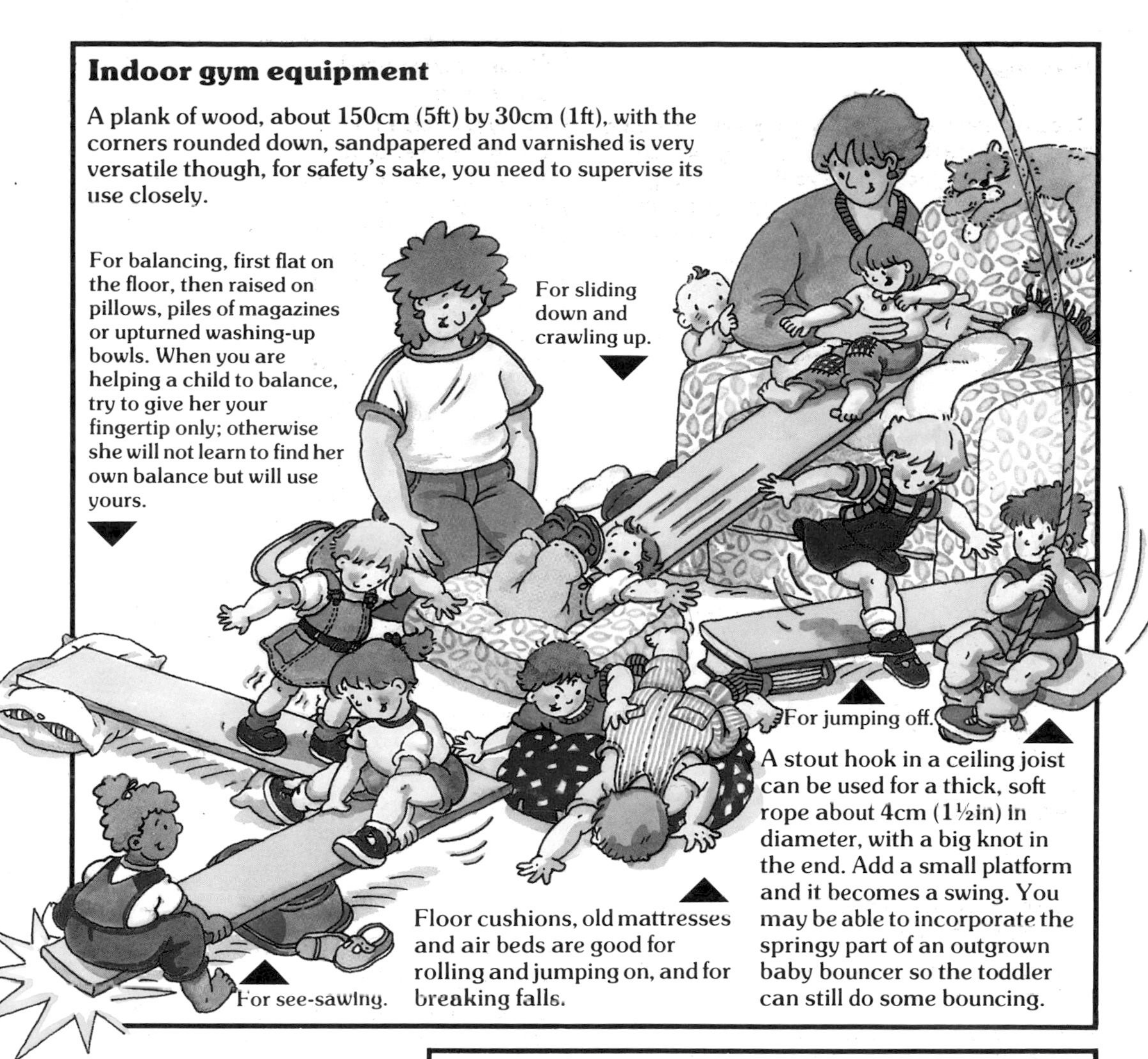

For balancing, first flat on the floor, then raised on pillows, piles of magazines or upturned washing-up bowls. When you are helping a child to balance, try to give her your fingertip only; otherwise she will not learn to find her own balance but will use yours.

For sliding down and crawling up.

For jumping off.

For see-sawing.

Floor cushions, old mattresses and air beds are good for rolling and jumping on, and for breaking falls.

A stout hook in a ceiling joist can be used for a thick, soft rope about 4cm (1½in) in diameter, with a big knot in the end. Add a small platform and it becomes a swing. You may be able to incorporate the springy part of an outgrown baby bouncer so the toddler can still do some bouncing.

Balls and bean bags

Toddlers are too young for proper ball games and cannot usually catch but they like throwing, fetching balls for you to throw, kicking large balls and may enjoy skittles and passing a ball through a hoop.

For a change from balls, you could make a bean bag. Make a bag about $13cm^2$ ($5in^2$) out of strong cotton, fill it with beans and sew it up securely all round.

Safety

Once a baby becomes mobile, extra safety precautions are essential. Here are just a few things to bear in mind.

★ Keep all exterior doors and gates shut, and if necessary locked, so the baby cannot get out.
★ Make sure he cannot lock himself in the bathroom or freezer.
★ Use safety gates across the top and bottom of the stairs.
★ Put fireguards round fires and fix them to the walls.
★ Put safety plugs in empty sockets.
★ Keep harmful substances and dangerous objects high up where the baby cannot reach them even by climbing. These include bleach and other cleaning fluids, medicines, alcohol, perfumes, tools, razors, scissors, knives, pins and needles, matches, plastic bags.
★ Turn saucepan handles inwards so they do not stick out over the edges of the cooker, or use a cooker guard.
★ Don't leave hot drinks or food where the baby can get them.
★ Always use a harness in baby chairs, pram and pushchair.

MESSY PLAY

Play that can be described broadly as "messy" has a useful function to perform for babies and toddlers. It is important to avoid the idea that getting messy is naughty, as this restricts a child's range of experience so much. Instead, concentrate on ways of keeping the mess within limits. Careful preparation for this sort of play can help. If you cannot bear mess, it is best not to attempt the most messy activities, however much you feel you should. You both need to be relaxed for the play to be enjoyable. Children perceive mess differently from adults but the more cautious are often wary of new textures and sensations and dislike getting dirty themselves.

The activities on the following pages can play an important part in increasing the strength and control of the hand and arm muscles and in developing co-ordination between hand and eye. They also provide opportunities to learn about the feel and texture of different materials and to form early concepts of size, shape, colour, quantity and capacity.

In a more general sense, they can stimulate the imagination and creativity, give a sense of achievement, and help to develop powers of observation, concentration and communication. Last but not least, many of these activities can be extremely soothing and relaxing.

Playing with paint

First painting sessions with toddlers are really just an opportunity to explore and play with paint. Children who enjoy mess will be happy to start "painting" very early. Those who are more wary of it may prefer to wait until they can hold and control a brush. It is probably worth having at least one experimental painting session by the time a child is two.

Protective covering. If you have to worry about where the paint is going, it will take a lot of the fun out of painting sessions, so it is worth providing good protection for clothes and the painting area.

For overalls you can use an old shirt worn back to front with the sleeves cut down, a plastic mac cut down to size, or a carrier bag with the bottom cut out and the handles as shoulder straps. You can buy plastic cuffs from good toyshops to protect sleeves.

For table and floor covering, use thick layers of newspaper, plastic tablecloths or cheap polythene sheeting.

Drawing

Early scribble

Later scribble

You can give a baby crayons to play with before she is able to use them but you will have to teach her not to put them in her mouth (if necessary by taking them away each time she does it). She will probably be able to make marks on paper with them from about 15 months onwards.

Before the age of two-and-a-half, children do not do much more than scribble on paper, first in straight lines, then gradually making deliberate curves and circles as well.

Try to draw things for your child. Even if you are bad at drawing, you can devise a few very simple pictures, perhaps by copying from her early picture books. She will enjoy seeing images she recognizes appear on the page. When she starts to talk, she will probably give titles to her own scribbles, however unrecognizable these may be to you.

Paint. Use fairly thick paint to start with. This is easier to control than runny paint and the texture is more interesting.

You can buy poster paints, specially thick poster paints called finger paints, or make your own paint by adding a little powder paint or food colouring to a thick paste. For the paste use wallpaper glue (non-fungicidal) or flour and water, or one of the recipes on the right:

1 Mix together:
½ cup soapflakes (not soap powder),
½ cup cold water starch,
¾ cup cold water.

2 Dissolve 1 cup cornflour in a little water.
Add 1 litre (2 pints) boiling water.
Boil until thick.
Take off heat.
Beat in 1 cup soapflakes (not soap powder).

If you mix a little washing-up liquid into the paint, it will wash off furniture and clothes more easily.

To begin with, provide just one colour of paint. Later you can increase the colour range gradually both for variety and the fun of mixing colours together.

Put the paint into any unbreakable container that will not be knocked over too easily. Margarine and large ice cream tubs are good.

Painting surfaces. You do not need to provide large sheets of clean white paper for early painting sessions. You can use a conveniently-situated washable surface such as a plastic-coated worktop, a draining board or even a window. Trays and plastic-coated chopping boards make good surfaces. Many toddlers are happy to paint on newspaper to start with. The back of left-over wallpaper, and wall and shelf lining paper are also useful.

Things to paint with. To get a toddler started, try spreading paint over the surface you are using with a brush or sponge and showing him how to draw in it with his finger, a brush or a stick. You can also provide other things to make marks in the paint with, such as kitchen utensils or a comb.

Brushes should be fairly short and thick for easy holding. A small decorators' brush works quite well. When you start providing more than one colour of paint, try to have a brush for each colour.

Show the toddler how to make prints with her hands and other things such as cut up vegetables, a paper cup or a washable toy.

Crayons. The best type to provide at first are short, fat, non-toxic wax ones. They are the easiest to hold, do not break easily and do not require too much pressure on the paper. Ordinary crayons can be a little sharp and dangerous if carried around. Don't let babies or toddlers play with lead pencils unless you can ensure they do not suck them.

Paper. Build up a supply of scrap paper, for example used envelopes opened out, used wrapping paper and other packaging. It might be worth asking local offices if they have any scrap paper you could have.

You may need to stick the paper to the surface underneath to hold it steady.

Always bring out paper with crayons and put them away together if you want to avoid drawing on walls and furniture.

Playing with water

Where to play. The best place for indoor water play is the bath, where spills can be kept to a minimum. Start bath play early – pouring water for the baby to watch, making gentle splashes and, once he can sit up, giving him things to play with. The happier he is in water, the more likely he is to enjoy going swimming (see pages 36-37). Remember that bath play does not have to be restricted to "bathtime" but can be a good way of relaxing or cheering up a baby at any time of day.

Toddlers often enjoy standing on a chair by the sink, washbasin or a baby bath on a stand. You can buy plastic toddler basins which fit to the side of the bath. These can be ideal for water play.

Alternatively, put a washing-up bowl or large plastic dish on the floor. Only put a small amount of water in it until the baby has learnt not to tip it straight out on to the floor. Put old towels or cloths down to absorb spills.

If you want to prevent clothes getting wet, you will have to take them off or provide wellingtons and plastic macs or aprons. Plastic cuffs will help to keep sleeves dry.

In warm weather, bowls, buckets, hosepipes and sprinklers are great fun in a garden and an inflatable paddling pool is a good investment.

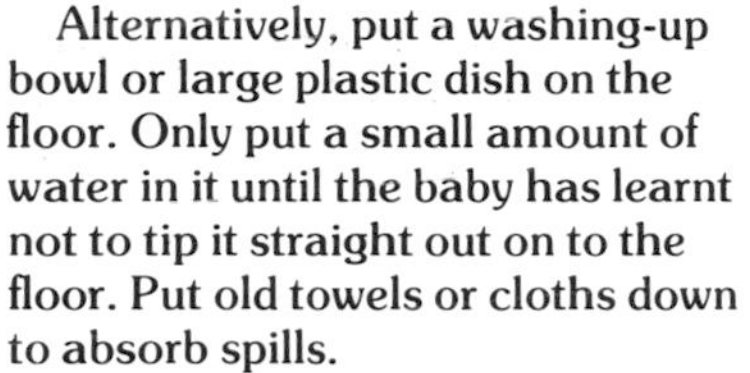

Things to play with. Besides proper bath toys, you can provide things from the kitchen such as plastic cups and jugs, spoons, a ladle, strainer, colander, funnel and an empty plastic bottle with holes made in it (use a heated metal knitting needle).

For a change, colour the water with food colouring or paint.

Once a toddler enjoys imitating adults, suggest bathing dolls or washing up plastic cups and plates. Outdoors, provide a cloth and bucket for washing cars and tricycles, or a paint brush and bucket for "painting" walls.

Bubbles. Make bubbles by blowing down straws into water, squeezing empty detergent bottles or mixing one part washing-up liquid with two parts water and blowing through a bent wire or bought plastic bubble blower.

Playing with sand

You do not need to have a sandpit in order to provide sand play. Just put a small amount of sand in an old washing-up bowl or baby bath, or fill an old tyre. Buy silver sand rather than builders' sand which stains clothes and skin.

Dry sand behaves rather like water so many of the containers used for water play are also suitable for sand. Toddlers may also enjoy sweeping it with a broom or dustpan and brush, weighing it on a set of balance scales or simply filling an assortment of containers with it.

Mixing sand and water together and moulding the wet sand into shape is fun. Pastry cutters, jelly moulds and foil or polystyrene food packaging all make good sand moulds.

Safety and hygiene

- ★ Babies and toddlers can drown in very small amounts of water. Never leave them alone with it, even for a moment.
- ★ Cover hot taps with strips of towelling.
- ★ Clean sand by rinsing it with water containing baby bottle sterilizer. Cover sand kept outdoors.
- ★ If sand gets in someone's eyes, rinse them with cold water.

Playdough

Making playdough. You can buy playdough but it is a good deal cheaper to make it. The basic ingredients are flour and water. The recipe on the right makes a dough that has a pliable texture and will keep for several months in an airtight container in the fridge.

For variety, you could add food colouring or paint either to the water or at the kneading stage.

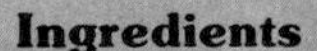

Ingredients

2 teaspoons cream of tartar
1 cup plain flour
½ cup salt
1 tablespoon oil
1 cup water

Mix to form a smooth paste. Put in a saucepan and cook slowly, until the dough comes away from the side of the pan and forms a ball. When it is cool enough, take the dough out of the pan and knead for three to four minutes. Put the pan to soak immediately.

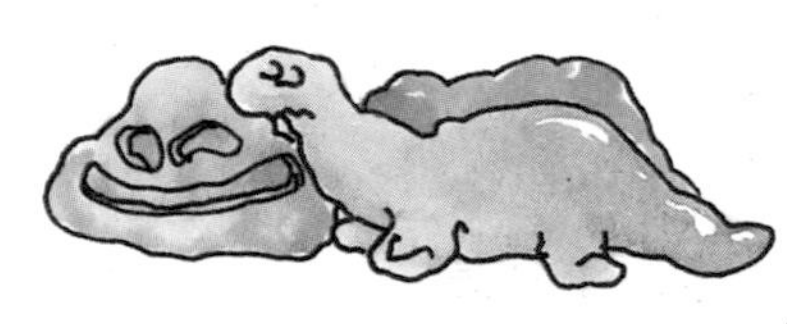

Playing with playdough. It is worth seeing how a toddler reacts to playdough at about 18 months, perhaps earlier if you can stop her eating it. Show her how to squeeze and squash it into different shapes and make things for her.

Later you can give her some tools with which to make marks in it and cut it. Try plastic cutlery, lolly sticks and, when she no longer puts things in her mouth, bottle caps.

Playdough can be very useful when you are cooking. Give her some safe kitchen utensils and containers so she can imitate you.

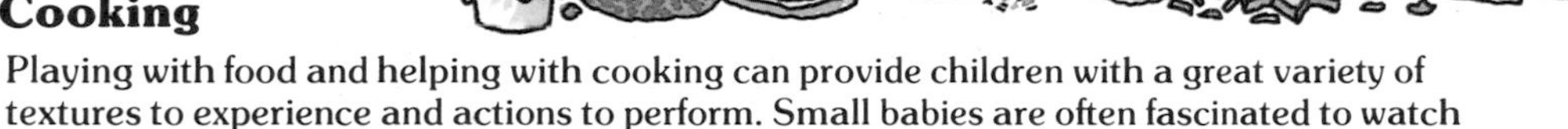

Cooking

Playing with food and helping with cooking can provide children with a great variety of textures to experience and actions to perform. Small babies are often fascinated to watch cooking in progress; later they enjoy playing with kitchen utensils and vegetables.

At the stage when a toddler can control a spoon and wants to imitate the things he sees going on in the kitchen, you could try giving him a large bowl of pasta, oats or rice with a spoon and some smaller containers to put the food into.

Stirring and mixing are really the first useful things toddlers can do to help with cooking. Yoghurt dishes are a good idea. Just provide some raisins, chopped fruit, ground nuts, jam or honey to mix into it. Some people find instant mix cakes, biscuits and desserts give toddlers satisfying results while being very simple to make. If you put a damp cloth under the mixing bowl, it will stop it slipping.

Cutting can be mastered surprisingly early if you start with soft foods like bananas, bread or large, flat mushrooms and use a blunt knife for safety. It is worth having an assortment of pastry cutters for cutting out biscuits and scones.

Decorating dishes makes food seem more interesting to children and makes them feel they have had a big hand in the preparation.

Safety and hygiene

- ★ Get together all you need before you start cooking, so you do not need to leave your child unsupervised.
- ★ Teach children to wash their hands before cooking.
- ★ Teach them to be careful when handling knives.
- ★ Teach them to ask before tasting anything.
- ★ If you spill something, clear it up promptly. One of you might slip on it.
- ★ Don't let children touch electric appliances or the cooker. Turn pan handles inwards or use a cooker guard.

IMITATING AND PRETENDING

Babies can imitate other people during their first year, and learn some of their earliest skills this way, but it is not until they are into their second year that pretending really begins. To pretend, they must be able to remember things they have seen happen and to imagine that one thing is really another. Picking up a spare rag and helping someone clean the car is imitating. Taking a tea towel from the kitchen and wiping it over a toy truck is pretending.

Make-believe usually starts around the time a baby begins to talk. This type of play, and the talking aloud that often accompanies it, actually helps toddlers to learn to think and sort out ideas. It helps them begin to imagine how it feels to be other people and allows them to experiment with emotions of, say, an aggressive nature which in real life might be unacceptable or disturbing. In doing so, they can learn to come to terms with such emotions and to control them. In their fantasy play they are able to take charge of situations in which they would normally be powerless and this helps to build confidence. Make-believe can also be one of the more sociable types of play as children get older and so helps to develop social skills.

Make-believe is equally common and beneficial to both sexes and gives parents the opportunity to suggest reversals of the usual sex stereotypes, by giving boys dolls, for example, and encouraging girls to imitate do-it-yourself tasks.

The best role parents can play in imitating and pretending is to make casual demonstrations, such as building a tower of bricks or offering teddy a biscuit; to join in make-believe if invited, for example to be a guest at a tea party or have a telephone conversation; to provide the few props that are needed for this age group and to try to allay any fears that may arise if fantasy and reality occasionally become confused.

Early imitation

Very young babies may try to mimic facial expressions. Full facial expressions of mood are not inborn but are learnt by imitation. Later, a baby learns to copy actions, such as clapping, and sounds, such as coughing and, very importantly, speech.

New skills are often learnt by imitation, but keep any demonstrations very casual and don't press the point. The baby may imitate you if you imitate her first. If she lifts her hand, try lifting yours, then waving.

Dolls, soft toys and puppets

These can be of great emotional value. They take on different roles as their owner wishes and so provide an outlet for all types of feelings. They also encourage talking.

In general, the simpler the toys, the more they stimulate the imagination. They need to be soft enough to be cuddly and the right size to fit the child's arms comfortably. A first doll needs to be a baby that can have things done for it. Dolls that can be bathed are often liked and ones that are flexible can be dressed.

First dolls' clothes should be easy to take off, if not put on. Try hats, socks, mittens, bibs, unbuttoned jackets, skirts with elasticated waists, ponchos or cloaks with self-fastening tape at the neck.

You can make a simple hand puppet out of an old sock or mitten. Sew on beads or buttons for eyes and a nose, and felt for a tongue, or embroider them in wool, perhaps adding woolly hair. For finger puppets see page 15 and for a wooden spoon puppet see page 6.

Around the house

By about a year old, babies are wanting to imitate the household tasks they see going on around them. Letting a toddler "help" will certainly slow you down but will give him a lot of pleasure, teach him new skills, develop his use of language and build his confidence. From a parent's point of view, there is something to be said for starting to teach toddlers how to be genuinely useful while they still see this as play rather than a chore. They often enjoy helping to:

unpack shopping
load and unload the washing machine
dust, polish and wipe up spills
sweep and wash floors
wash up (see page 28)
cook (see page 29)
make beds
tidy up toys
wash the car
dig the garden
decorate and do-it-yourself*

The toddler will almost certainly prefer using small-sized real tools to toy versions. These work more efficiently in any case but make sure they are safe.

Don't forget to provide encouragement by praising his accomplishments however small these may be.

This type of imitating soon shades into pretending. Most early fantasy play revolves around the home and the roles played by the people in it because this age group has only a limited experience of the outside world.

Useful props include:
Dolls, soft toys and puppets (see opposite)
The tools used for the household tasks mentioned above
The things listed on pages 10-11 under "Ideas for things to hold", especially –
plastic cups, saucers, plates and cutlery
metal teapot
metal kettle
saucepans

Dens

Toddlers often like having a den to hide and play in, usually in a corner of the room where you are. Drape an old sheet, blanket or curtain over a table, a framework of chairs or, outside, over a low washing line.

Dressing up

This age group cannot really cope with dressing-up clothes though older toddlers may like a cloak made from interestingly-textured and brightly-coloured material. You could cut down an old curtain (make sure it is not long enough to trip over), pull the gathering string up tight, cut off the loose ends, then sew on self-fastening tape.

Dressing-up accessories can be enjoyed from an early age. Hats and bags are most popular but you could also provide:

Jewellery (Dip macaroni into water containing food colouring, leave to dry, then thread on shirring elastic.)
Gloves
Shawls
Stoles (safer than long scarves)
Parasol
Apron
Purse

A mirror helps toddlers to develop a sense of self and so progress to imagining themselves as someone else.

Cardboard boxes

These can play a versatile role in make-believe, representing anything from vehicles and buildings to furniture.

Paper plate
Dowelling
Car
Cheese box
Cotton reels
Red felt pen
Cooker

*With all these activities around the house, be very conscious of safety. See pages 12, 25, 28 and 29.

THINGS TO FIT TOGETHER AND TAKE APART

Sometime during the first half of the second year babies seem to enter a new phase of intense curiosity about the objects that surround them. They want to know what they can do, how they work and how their own actions affect them. They start experimenting with things to see what will happen, to solve puzzles and to achieve certain goals. They need activities and toys to satisfy and encourage this curiosity, which will help them to develop both physical skills and important new thinking skills.

The activities and toys described on the next few pages advance and refine the manipulative skills that have been developing since the baby's early months. They improve hand/eye co-ordination and strengthen the hand and arm muscles to allow for much finer hand control and delicate finger movements.

Handling objects and experimenting with what they can do helps children learn to identify similarities and differences between objects, to match like with like and to discover group identities. This is a very important step forward and leads, at about the age of two, to the ability to link information together to form mental concepts. The ability to think in this way is related to ability to use language and communicate.

During this period, bought toys really come into their own. Exact fit can be hard to achieve in home-made toys but is an important element in these activities and produces the most satisfying results. Manufacturers are also better able to make toys light, smooth and unbreakable. Nevertheless, home-made toys can be useful for introducing new ideas, finding out what a child likes and providing variety.

When you introduce a new toy, you may need to demonstrate its possibilities by playing with it casually yourself. Don't try to show a child what to do with it, though. Freedom to experiment is the main point of these activities.

Fitting

Simple toys which encourage babies to place objects accurately, the right way round and the right way up, often become popular around the first birthday. Remember that round shapes are the easiest to deal with at first.

Lids. Provide a variety of containers, including pans, with lids to fit on and take off. Egg poachers are often particularly enjoyed.

Shape sorters and posting boxes. There are many different types of these varying in difficulty. A shoe box can make a good first shape sorter. First cut a round hole in the lid, just the right size for a small ball. When the baby can post this, cut a brick-shaped hole, then gradually add other shapes. Later she will be able to post things like coins* and playing cards into slots.

You could introduce the idea of posting by demonstrating how to post a ping-pong ball down a kitchen or toilet roll tube.

Stacking

Beakers. A set of graded plastic beakers is an excellent stacking toy and can also be used for other purposes (see "Nesting toys" opposite).

Rings and balls. Plastic or wooden rings or balls stack on a central spindle, sometimes forming the shapes of people or animals.

Take care until the baby stops putting things in her mouth.

Nesting toys. A set of graded plastic beakers is the simplest and best nesting toy to start with and can be used for several other purposes too, for example emptying and filling, or stacking (see opposite). A set of plastic kitchen bowls might serve the same purpose. Paper cups and cake cases are fun for beginners but can be fitted together in any order and so are less challenging than sets of graded sizes. Plastic eggs and barrels, and traditional Russian dolls are more difficult to master but have a long play life.

First jigsaw puzzles. The simplest of these, sometimes called playtrays or inset boards, have pieces which have to be slotted into individual spaces. Some have knobs on each piece to make them easier to lift out. Others have pieces which can stand upright and be used for imaginative play. Some are helpful for learning about things like colours and sizes. Others can be used later as templates for drawing round.

For variety, you could make a simple playtray. Cut some simple shapes out of a piece of thick card, then stick the card to another piece of card the same size. Colour in or paint the pieces to make them look more interesting.

Turning and screwing

The wrist movement adults use automatically for all sorts of practical tasks takes quite a bit of practice to master. Activity centres usually include a turning device; musical toys that wind up and toys with keys to turn also give good practice. You can also buy rods with variously-shaped nuts to screw on to them.

The difficulty in devising your own wrist-movement toys is finding things that are not too small and fiddly. Plastic screw-topped jars and bottles*, nuts* and bolts, keys and locks are all good if you can find big enough ones. At a certain stage toddlers are often fascinated by doorknobs and taps.

You can improvise some stacking rings that are not size-graded.

Piece of dowelling stuck to hardboard base.

Cheese boxes with holes cut in centre.

Cut-up kitchen or toilet roll tube.

Napkin rings

Used rolls of adhesive tape.

Bangles

Plastic bottle stuck to hardboard.

Bricks. A set of bricks usually has a long play life and is used for simple stacking long before being used to construct walls, buildings or layouts. You need quite a lot of bricks for building proper so, if you buy only a few to begin with, make sure you will be able to add to them later. Make sure, too, that different-sized bricks are in scale (whole, halves, quarters). Wooden bricks are more expensive than plastic but last longer and are more satisfying to play with.

For early stacking, you can use tins and packets of food as well as bricks.

Threading

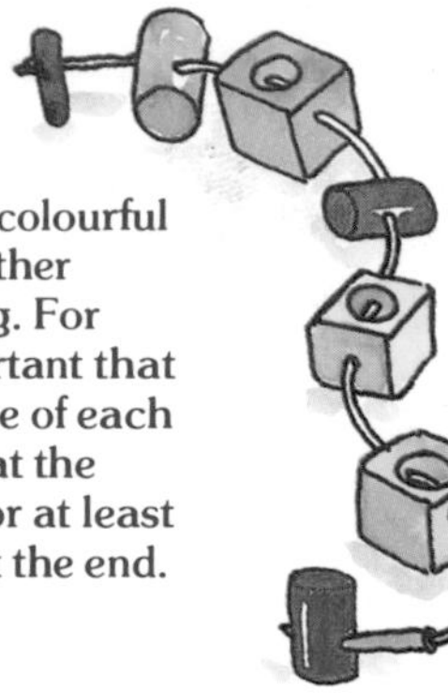

You can buy sets of colourful blocks, beads and other shapes for threading. For beginners it is important that the hole in the centre of each item is large and that the thread is fairly stiff or at least has a long stiff bit at the end.

You could try making your own threading toys from cut-up kitchen or toilet roll tubes, used small rolls of adhesive tape, curtain rings, or large nuts. For the thread use plastic or rubber tubing, or string attached at the end to a straw or piece of dowelling for stiffness.

You could also cut a simple shape out of card, make some large holes in it and tie on a threading device, as shown on the right.

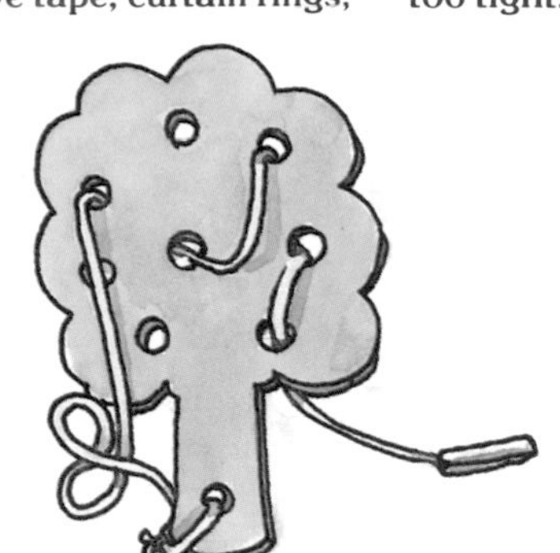

Hooks, poppers and zips

Although this age group cannot master the skills required for dressing and undressing, they can start practising some of the techniques involved. You can buy plastic chains that pop or hook together and dolls with zips, poppers and buttons. Old bags and purses can give good practice with zips. If you can sew, you could try making a cushion like the one shown below. Make the buttonholes large and don't sew the buttons on too tight.

Matching, grouping and grading

Many of the activities described on this and the previous two pages help children learn to match things according to their shape, size or colour. Finding two identical objects is the simplest sort of grouping.

You can help to develop this ability further by encouraging a child to put assortments of objects into groups.

You can encourage an awareness of relative size by helping a child to grade objects in size order.

Other things you could use for matching, grouping and grading include*:

Vegetables	Crayons
Pasta	Tiddlywinks
Plastic cutlery	Buttons
Bricks	Stones
Small toy animals	Shells

Construction toys

These are toys which require a combination of the fitting, stacking and screwing skills described on the last two pages. The term covers a wide range of toys from simple pull-apart vehicles to complicated building systems. Only the simplest building systems are really suitable for children under two-and-a-half.

**Take care with small objects if the child still puts things in his mouth.*

OUTINGS AND JOURNEYS

Babies and toddlers need frequent trips out to avoid boredom, to broaden their experience, to meet people and, once they can walk, for exercise. Outings also provide opportunities for developing language if you talk about what you see.

Going out can also be more enjoyable for a parent than trying to entertain a bored baby at home even though, for longish outings, you have to plan ahead where you could feed and change the baby and have to remember to take all the necessary equipment such as food, drink, nappies, toys and comforter.

If a very young baby likes being in a sling, you can take him almost anywhere without much difficulty. Older babies and toddlers cannot keep still for long and need to get out of their buggy or car seat regularly for a break.

Local outings

These may seem mundane to you but everything the baby sees is new and interesting and, because his attention span is short, he appreciates the constantly-changing scene. If he gets bored, tie toys to the buggy or give him some shopping to hold.

Once a baby can walk, he needs time to investigate everything you pass. (See page 24 for possible problems with walking out-of-doors.)

Ideas for outings

The kind of outings you go on obviously depends on your individual circumstances. The local paper and library are good places to look for information about any special events in your area. Here are a few simple, general ideas for places to go:

somewhere to watch trains, boats or aeroplanes
a short train, bus or car ride (whatever form of transport is unusual for you)
the outside of a police or fire station
a building site or roadworks
a car wash
a duckpond
a farm park
a zoo
a pet shop
a library
swimming (see pages 36-37)

Long journeys

Young babies are often lulled to sleep by the motion of travelling and it is sometimes worth planning journeys with older babies and toddlers to coincide with sleep times. You could also try these ideas:

★ Stick pictures on the backs of the front seats and the back doors.
★ Take along a varied selection of toys and introduce them a few at a time, perhaps loosely wrapped or in a bag for the baby to unpack. Tie toys to the baby's seat on short lengths of string.
★ Sing songs, recite nursery rhymes and play cassettes of these. Compile your own tapes of favourites.
★ Give small, frequent snacks of non-messy foods such as cheese, biscuits, carrot, apple, seedless grapes and sultanas.
★ Stop for about five minutes every hour for walkers to stretch their legs.

Socializing

Most babies love company and benefit from the attention and stimulation it gives them. They cannot understand the concepts of sharing or taking turns until they are about three and so cannot really play with other children until then, though they will happily play alongside so long as someone is there to keep the peace. Visiting friends with children and going to mother-and-toddler clubs provide invaluable opportunities for mixing with other children and starting to develop social skills.

GOING SWIMMING

There are several good reasons for taking babies and toddlers swimming. The most important is that they can get tremendous enjoyment from it; the younger they are, the less likely it is that they will be afraid of the water and strange places, and the more easily they will learn to swim; children with some experience of swimming are safer when playing in or near water; swimming is excellent all-round exercise and it can be a very sociable activity.

Opinions differ as to exactly what is the best age to start swimming sessions. Some people believe that after nine months in a fluid environment before birth, babies are born knowing how to swim and the sooner you introduce them to the water, the better. Spectacular results have been achieved with very small babies following specific methods.

However, many child care experts are unhappy about starting swimming too early because of the risk of cold and infection. Babies lose heat quickly and it is dangerous for them to get cold because their body heating mechanisms are less efficient than adults'. Some experts advise waiting until about six months, by which time babies' natural immunity is fairly well developed and they have had one, if not two, immunizations.

Developing confidence at home

The first step towards enjoying swimming is feeling confident in the water. A baby's first experience of water is bathtime so make this an unhurried, relaxing time for playing and splashing.

Bathing with a parent makes some babies feel more secure in the water and can be great fun for both.

When the baby can sit by himself, give him things to play with, including armbands.

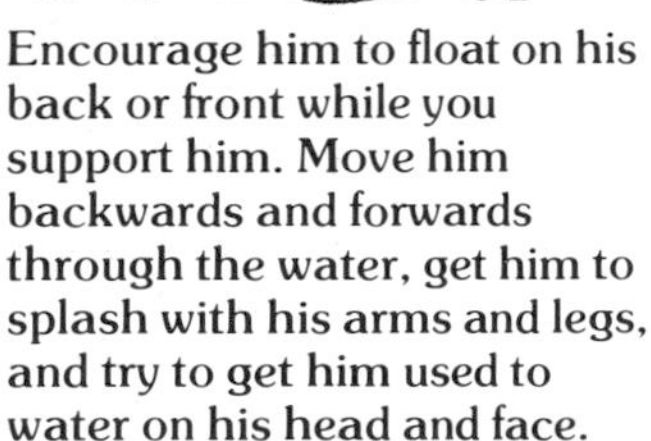

Encourage him to float on his back or front while you support him. Move him backwards and forwards through the water, get him to splash with his arms and legs, and try to get him used to water on his head and face.

A toddler can get some idea of what to expect at the swimming pool by looking at books about swimming and by trying on a costume or trunks, and armbands.

First visit to a swimming pool

On your first visit to a swimming pool, it is a good idea to have a look round without actually swimming. This gives the child a chance to get used to the strange atmosphere, noise and smell without the additional strangeness of getting undressed and going in the water.

Swimming pool facilities

It may be worth travelling a little further than you need to find a pool with really good facilities for babies and toddlers.

* What temperature is the water? It needs to be between 27°C (80°F) and 30°C (86°F) and for small babies should be at least 29°C (85°F). The air temperature should be one or two degrees above the water temperature.
* Are there changing mats or tables for dressing and undressing babies, and playpens to put them in while you get changed?
* Is there a separate pool for small children? It is very helpful to be away from the rough-and-tumble of the main pool.
* How do you get into the pool? Some toddlers would rather walk into the water than be carried. Wide, shallow steps or a gentle slope are safest.
* How deep is the shallow water? It is best if there is an area of very shallow water where a child can sit, crawl or splash about.
* Are there classes for parents and children? These are an excellent idea especially if you yourself are not very confident in the water. If not, when is the pool quietest?

In the water

Your general aim is to get your child to feel confident and enjoy himself in the water. Keep each session short (10-20 minutes is long enough for this age group) but go to the pool frequently.

Hold your child close, with your head on a level with hers. Keeping eye contact, gently sink into the water up to your shoulders.

When he seems happy, hold him away from you, bounce him up and down, and move him backwards and forwards through the water.

Lay him on his back, supporting him under his hips with one hand, under his neck with the other.

Lay her on her front, supporting her under her chest with one hand, under her hips with the other.

Tow her along, holding her by her fingertips and encouraging her to kick her legs.

When she seems confident, let go for a few seconds. If she is reluctant, get her to pat a ball along.

When she is happy to move independently through the the water, encourage her to change direction and turn from her front to her back.

Ger her used to splashes on her face and head, then encourage her to put first her face, then her whole head, in the water.*

Make this very brief. The reason children can drown so easily is that they do not know to hold their breath in water but automatically open their mouths to cry.

Armbands and toys

It is probably worth buying armbands from about six months. Buy the ones with double chambers and safety valves, and check for punctures before each session. Make sure they are small enough to stay on: they should be worn above the elbow. You can gradually reduce the amount of air in them until they are no longer needed. Many children refuse to wear them at first but, if allowed just to play with them, usually consent in the end. Nervous babies may appreciate a ring as well as armbands, but don't use a ring alone as babies can slip through them. At the end of each session, have a few minutes without floating aids, so the baby gets used to the feel of managing without them.

Taking things like boats, beach balls, watering cans and bath toys to the pool helps to make babies feel more at home.

Hygiene and safety

★ Dress babies who are not potty-trained in close-fitting pants.
★ Watch out for slippery floors.
★ Teach toddlers to go to the toilet, blow their nose and go under the shower before getting in the water.
★ If you have to climb down a ladder into the pool, hand the baby to someone else while you do so. Teach toddlers to climb down backwards.
★ Always supervise young children closely even if they can swim quite well. Be especially careful with older children around.
★ Take a towel to the pool-side and wrap babies up as soon as they get out. Dress them warmly.
★ Don't take a child swimming if he has a cold or seems even slightly unwell.

MUSIC, SONGS AND RHYMES

From the earliest weeks of life, babies find gentle music and singing soothing and relaxing. As they get older, they seem to like music with strong rhythms best. You can buy a variety of tapes, usually of nursery rhymes and songs, that are specially compiled to appeal to very young children.

Early exposure to many different types of music helps to develop babies' listening ability besides their capacity to enjoy music. Later, you can encourage them to follow their natural inclination to respond to music with movement and sounds of their own. Being sung to can also play an important part in both a baby's social and linguistic development.

Moving to music

Older babies and toddlers respond spontaneously to music they like by swaying and dancing. You can encourage this and help them to let off steam by joining in.

Mirror dancing. Put some music on and dance together in front of a long mirror.

Mood dances. Do happy, sad, fierce or jolly dances. Toddlers usually find this amusing and it helps them begin to understand different emotions and feelings. You could also try alternating fast and slow dancing or dance like different characters such as a clown, a witch or a giant.

Developing an awareness of sound

You can help a baby to learn to listen and become more aware of sound by drawing her attention to different everyday sounds and talking about them. Try pointing out the ticking of a clock, the rustle of leaves, rain falling, birds singing or an aeroplane going overhead. (See also "Things to listen to" on page 7.)

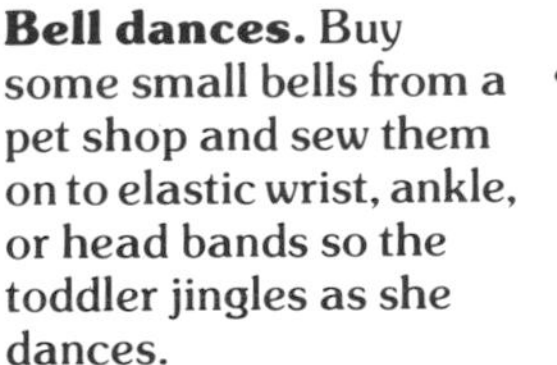

Bell dances. Buy some small bells from a pet shop and sew them on to elastic wrist, ankle, or head bands so the toddler jingles as she dances.

First instruments

Babies and toddlers enjoy joining in with music to make their own musical sounds. First instruments consist mainly of things to shake and things to bang.

Things to shake. Rattles are really a baby's first instruments. For suggestions for home-made rattles see page 7. Below are a few more ideas for "shakers".*

Jingle bells. Screw a ring hook into the end of a thick piece of dowelling and tie small bells to it.

Maracas. Put some pasta into two strong paper bags and fasten them to dowelling with string.

Tambourine. Fasten foil bottle tops round the edge of a paper plate with thread as shown below.

Things to bang. Try giving these to the baby from about six months. Saucepans, cake tins, plastic bowls and buckets, and coffee tins with plastic lids all make good drums when hit with a wooden or metal spoon. To make drumheads, tie greaseproof paper over them.

Songs and rhymes with actions

Babies and toddlers love being sung to and some experts believe that this can play an important part in the "bonding" process between baby and parent. Sing or chant any songs that you enjoy yourself: nursery rhymes, lullabies, pop or folk songs, using tapes to help you if necessary.

Action rhymes and songs are a valuable form of entertainment for babies from about six months. The actions help to hold the baby's attention and, later, to convey the meaning of the words. Babies also enjoy the physical and social interaction involved and learn to anticipate the actions. The more energetic songs encourage body control and provide opportunities to use up surplus energy. The actions to the rhymes given below and on the next two pages are printed in the lighter type.**

This little pig went to market,
This little pig stayed at home;
This little pig had roast beef,
This little pig had none.
And this little pig cried,
"Wee-wee-wee,
I can't find my way home."

(Wiggle each of the baby's toes in turn, starting with the big one, and on the last line run fingers up baby's leg and tickle tummy.)

Round and round the garden,
Like a teddy bear;
One step, two step,
Tickly under there!

(Run finger round baby's palm. On the third line, jump finger up her arm and tickle armpit.)

Knock at the door,
(Tap forehead.)
Pull the bell,
(Tug lock of hair.)
Lift up the latch,
(Pinch tip of nose upwards.)
Walk in.
(Poke finger into mouth.)
Chin chopper, chin chopper,
(Tap under chin.)
Chin, chin, chin.
(Tickle under chin.)

Cobbler, cobbler, mend my shoe,
(Bang fists together.)
Get it done by half past two.
(Shake finger bossily.)
'Cos my toe is peeping through,
(Push right thumb through left fist and wiggle.)
Cobbler, cobbler, mend my shoe.
(Bang fists together.)

One, two, three, four, five,
(Count on fingers.)
Once I caught a fish alive.
(Wiggle hand to look like a fish.)
Six, seven, eight, nine, ten,
(Count on fingers.)
Then I let him go again.
(Pretend to throw fish back.)
Why did you let him go?
Because he bit my finger so.
(Shake hand as though in pain.)
Which finger did he bite?
This little finger on the right.
(Hold up little finger on right hand.)

Pat-a-cake, pat-a-cake, baker's man,
Bake me a cake as fast as you can.
Pat it and prick it and mark it with B,
And put it in the oven for baby and me.

(Clap hands in rhythm. On the third line, pretend to prick palm of baby's hand and draw a B on it. On the fourth line, pretend to put cake in oven.)

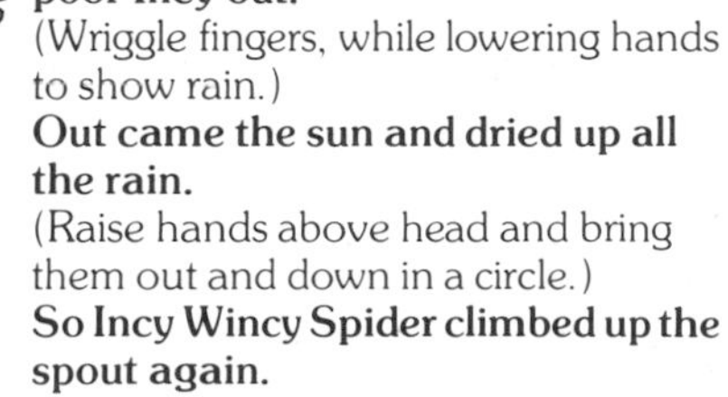

Incy Wincy Spider, climbing up the spout.
(Use fingers to show spider climbing upwards.)
Down came the rain and washed poor Incy out.
(Wriggle fingers, while lowering hands to show rain.)
Out came the sun and dried up all the rain.
(Raise hands above head and bring them out and down in a circle.)
So Incy Wincy Spider climbed up the spout again.
(Repeat climbing action.)

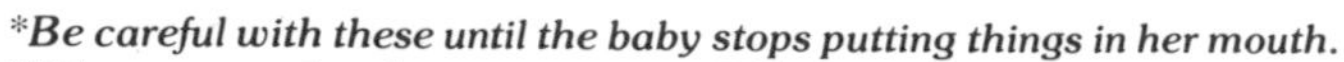

***Be careful with these until the baby stops putting things in her mouth.**
*****For more action rhymes see pages 71 and 72.***

Clap, clap hands, one, two, three,
Put your hands upon your knees,
Lift them high to touch the sky,
Clap, clap hands and away they fly.

(Follow actions described.)

Baby's shoes,
Mummy's shoes,
Daddy's shoes,
Policeman's shoes,
Giant's shoes!

(Show length of each pair of shoes by holding hands apart. Hands become wider and wider apart.)

The elephant walks
Like this and that.
(Part knees and rock from side to side.)
He's terribly tall
(Hold hands up high.)
And terribly fat.
(Hold hands out wide.)
He's got no fingers,
(Wriggle fingers.)
He's got no toes.
(Touch toes.)
But goodness, gracious,
What a nose!
(Wave arm in front of face like a trunk.)

Row, row, row your boat,
Gently down the stream,
Merrily, merrily, merrily, merrily,
Life is but a dream.

(Rock backwards and forwards in rowing action.)

I'm a little teapot, short and stout,
Here's my handle,
(Put hand on hip.)
Here's my spout.
(Hold out other arm, bent at elbow and wrist.)
When I get the steam up, hear me shout,
"Tip me up and pour me out."
(Bend over to side of "spout", as though being poured.)

I hear thunder, I hear thunder;
(Clap hands or stamp foot in rhythm.)
Hark, don't you? Hark, don't you?
(Cup hand to ear.)
Pitter-patter raindrops,
Pitter-patter raindrops,
(Wriggle fingers to show rain.)
I'm wet through.
(Feel clothes, then wring hands.)
So are you!
(Point to baby.)

Jack in the box is a funny wee man,
Sits in his box as still as he can . . .
Then up he pops!

(Crouch down and jump up on last line.)

Eight big fingers standing up tall,
Two big ears to hear mummy call,
One little nose to blow and blow,
Ten little toes in a wiggly row,
Two fat thumbs that wiggle up and down,
Two little feet to stand on the ground.
Hands to clap and eyes to see,
Oh, what fun to be just me.

(Indicate each part of the body mentioned.)

Clap your hands, clap your hands,
Clap them just like me.

Touch your shoulders, touch your shoulders,
Touch them just like me.

Tap your knees, tap your knees,
Tap them just like me.

Shake your head, shake your head,
Shake it just like me.

Clap your hands, clap your hands,
Then let them quiet be.

(Follow actions described.)

Teddy bear, teddy bear dance on your toes.
Teddy bear, teddy bear touch your nose.
Teddy bear, teddy bear stand on your head.
Teddy bear, teddy bear go to bed.
Teddy bear, teddy bear wake up now.
Teddy bear, teddy bear make a bow.

(Follow actions described.)

This is the way the lady rides,
Trit, trot, trit, trot, trit, trot.

This is the way the gentleman rides,
A-gallop, a-gallop, a-gallop, a-gallop.

This is the way the farmer rides,
Hobbledy, hobbledy, hobbledy, hobbledy,

And into the ditch!

(Jiggle baby up and down on knee in different riding actions and on the last line pretend to let her fall off.)

To market, to market,
To buy a fat pig;
Home again, home again,
Jiggety jig.

To market, to market,
To buy a fat hog;
Home again, home again,
Joggety jog.

(Jiggle baby up and down on knee in time to rhythm.)

This little bird flaps its wings,
Flaps its wings, flaps its wings,
This little bird flaps its wings
And flies away in the morning!

(Interlock thumbs and flap outstretched fingers, lifting hands higher and higher.)

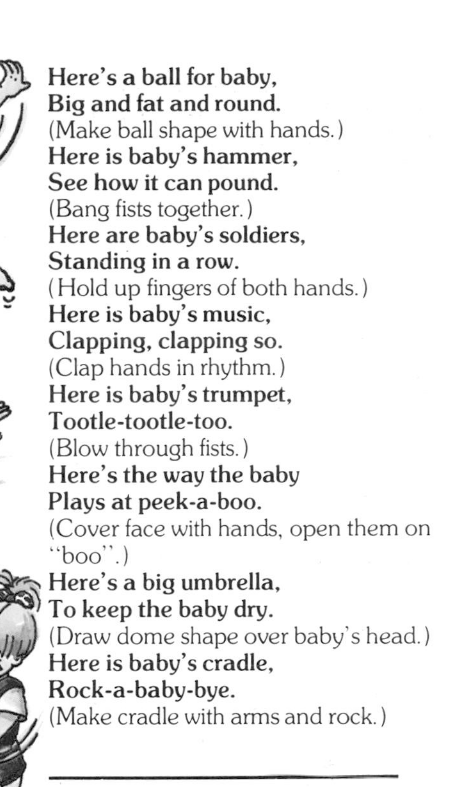

Here's a ball for baby,
Big and fat and round.
(Make ball shape with hands.)
Here is baby's hammer,
See how it can pound.
(Bang fists together.)
Here are baby's soldiers,
Standing in a row.
(Hold up fingers of both hands.)
Here is baby's music,
Clapping, clapping so.
(Clap hands in rhythm.)
Here is baby's trumpet,
Tootle-tootle-too.
(Blow through fists.)
Here's the way the baby
Plays at peek-a-boo.
(Cover face with hands, open them on "boo".)
Here's a big umbrella,
To keep the baby dry.
(Draw dome shape over baby's head.)
Here is baby's cradle,
Rock-a-baby-bye.
(Make cradle with arms and rock.)

Ring a ring o' roses,
A pocket full of posies,
A-tishoo, a-tishoo,
We all fall down.

The king has sent his daughter
To fetch a pail of water,
A-tishoo, a-tishoo,
We all fall down.

The robin on the steeple
Is singing to the people,
A-tishoo, a-tishoo,
We all fall down.

(Hold hands and skip round in a circle, falling down on last line of each verse.)

GUIDE TO STAGES OF DEVELOPMENT

It can be useful to have some idea of the age at which babies and toddlers are likely to reach certain stages of development so that you can provide the encouragement and opportunity to practise new skills at the right time.

However, while babies and toddlers tend to go through the different stages of development in the same order, for example, learning to roll over before they learn to sit up, in reality there is a wide variation in the rate at which they go through the stages. For instance, learning to walk at any time between nine and 18 months is perfectly normal, although the average age is 13 months. For this reason, many of the developments described below and on the next few pages have been listed within fairly broad age bands. Where a lot of developments take place during a certain period, more specific ages have been given but these should be taken as a rough guide only.

The difference in the rate of development of different babies is accounted for not only by physical maturity, intellectual ability and the amount of stimulation received from the environment but also by personality. Rapid early development seems to bear very little relation to ability later in life.

It is also worth remembering that rapid progress in one area of development may temporarily slow down progress in another area. For example, learning to walk often slows down language development for a while.

Stage*	General physical development	Using eyes	Using hands
Birth	•Baby's position is all curled up. •When on front, can lift head just enough to turn it from one side to other. •When lifted up, head flops because neck muscles are not strong enough to support it.	•Only sees clearly things about 25cm (10in) from nose. •Everything looks rather two-dimensional. •Responds to bright colours. •Turns towards moderately bright sources of light. •Briefly follows object dangled about 25cm (10in) from nose.	•Hands are held in a fist. •Grasps objects placed in palm but this is only a reflex action.
6 weeks	•On front, can hold head up for a few seconds. •Can be propped up in sitting position with cushions or pillows.	•Watches faces intently when held in arms.	
3 months	•Body uncurled. Arms and legs free. •Lies on back with back of head on mattress. •Kicks vigorously. •Raises head when pulled into sitting position. •Rolls from back to side and from side to back. •Holds head steady when held upright.	•Follows adults' movements. •Follows object dangled 25cm (10in) from nose, both from side to side and up and down. •Watches movement of own hands.	•Hands held open. •Plays with hands. •Swipes at hanging objects. •Can briefly hold objects placed in hands but does not yet look at them.

Remember that individual babies are unlikely to reach the stages at the precise ages given above. The ages are averages only.

The ages given for the toys and activities listed in the chart indicate when a baby or toddler is likely to start enjoying them for their main purpose. Some toys can be used in several different ways and so appeal to a wide range of ages. This is something to bear in mind, especially when buying toys. The more versatile the toy, the more it is likely to be played with and the better value it will be. Nesting beakers are one of the best examples of this and have something to offer over almost the whole age range covered by this book. Young babies enjoy holding and examining them, then they can be played with in the bath, later they are used for nesting, a little later still for stacking and eventually are helpful for colour matching.

If you introduce a toy to a baby and she does not appear interested in it, even after a casual demonstration, just put it away and try again a few weeks or months later. Although you can provide the encouragement and opportunity to learn through play, you cannot force progress or impose your own tastes. A baby has personal preferences just like older people and may never be particularly interested in certain types of toy, no matter what stage of development she has reached.

Listening and talking	**Doing things for self**	**Suitable toys and activities**
• Aware of surrounding noise, especially voices. • Startled by sudden loud noises. • Cries. 	 • Cries to make needs known.	• For the first few weeks of life, babies probably have enough to cope with just getting used to their new and totally strange environment. They need plenty of reassuring physical contact, gentle voices to listen to and faces to look at.
• Probably recognizes mother's voice. • Smiles at soothing voice. • Mimics talking by opening and closing mouth. • Gurgles.		• Things to look at (see pages 4-6). • Things to listen to (page 7). • Bouncing chair. • Massage (page 8). • Exercises (page 21). • Encourage to support own head (page 22).
• Turns towards sounds. • Can tell difference between one speech sound and another. • Chuckles. 		• Things to swipe at (see pages 8-9). • Things to kick (page 9). • Things to hold (pages 9-11), especially rattles. • Encourage rolling (page 22). 

Stage*	General physical development	Using eyes	Using hands
4 months	• On front, lifts head and shoulders, taking weight on arms and hands.  • Starts to roll from front to back. • If you support arms, can hold a sitting position.	• Can focus on objects at almost any distance.	• May try to take hold of things after measuring distance from hand by glancing backwards and forwards between the two.
6 months	• Raises head when lying on back.  • Rolls from back to front. • May sit unsupported for a few seconds. • Bounces up and down when held upright with feet touching a firm surface.	• Watches toy dropped where can see it. If falls out of sight, forgets about it.	• Picks up either with both hands or one, using palmar grasp.  • Transfers objects from one hand to other. • Puts everything in mouth. Grasps and plays with feet.
8 months	• May move around by rolling over and over. • Can sit unsupported if keeps still. • Gets into crawling position, and rocks backwards and forwards but cannot actually move along.	• Recognizes familiar faces.	• May offer things to people but cannot let go on purpose.
9 months	• Can reach for toys when sitting.  • Can get into sitting position from lying down. • Crawls. May move backwards at first because arms are stronger and better co-ordinated than legs. • Pulls self up to standing position, using people or furniture. Can take weight on feet but cannot balance.	 • Searches for toy dropped out of sight or hidden while watching.	• Starts to gain control over each finger separately and learns to poke and point.  • Waves bye-bye. • Claps hands. • Uses pincer grip (finger and thumb). Can pick up very small objects this way and pull a toy on a string towards him by grasping string.
11 months	• Can sit down from standing position, using furniture.  • Walks sideways, holding on to furniture. • Walks forwards if hands are held or when pushing baby walker.		• Learns to let go of things deliberately, then to throw and place them.  • Uses objects to empty and fill containers.

Remember that individual babies are unlikely to reach the stages at the precise ages given above. The ages are averages only.

Listening and talking	Doing things for self	Suitable toys and activities
 • Makes cooing noises: at first long vowel sounds, later adding first consonants. These early sounds are identical to all human babies. They are not trying to name anyone. • Blows raspberries.	• Puts hand to breast or bottle when feeding.	 • Things to grasp (see pages 10-11). • Bouncing on knee.
• Carries on "conversations" with an adult, making a sound, pausing for other person to reply, then answering. • Gradually stops making speech sounds that do not form part of the language she hears.		 • Picture books. • Encourage sitting (page 22). • Activity centre. • Bath toys. • Things to bang, e.g. drum, saucepan lid. • Baby bouncer (page 24). • Baby walker (page 24). • Swimming (pages 36-37).
 • Babbles in repetitive strings of syllables. • Shouts to attract attention. • Responds to own name. • Takes interest in adult conversation, even when not directly aimed at her.	 • Holds, bites and chews biscuit.	• Encourage crawling (see page 23). • Encourage understanding of words (page 15). 
• Understands a few words, e.g. no, bye-bye. • Joins up a variety of different sounds into "sentences". Practises different intonation patterns. 	 • Grabs spoon when being fed.	• Encourage standing (see page 23). • Small things to pick up (page 12). • Songs and rhymes with actions (pages 39-41). 
 • Uses first words. These are nearly always labels for people or things and may be made up. • Uses voice to draw attention to objects or events, or to get help in doing something or getting something.		• Encourage walking (see page 24). • Baby walker (push-along type). • Nesting beakers. • Letting go and droppping games (page 13). • Asking games (page 17). • Things to empty and fill (page 13).

Stage*	General physical development	Using eyes	Using hands
12-15 months	• Can lie down from sitting position without having to get on to all fours first. • Stands unsupported. Learns to walk a step between gaps in furniture, then to take first steps alone. • Crawls upstairs. 	 • Recognizes objects in books.	 • Can hold two objects in one hand.
15-18 months	• Walks steadily for short distances. • Gets to feet without pulling self up on furniture and sits down without using furniture. • Climbs into adults' chairs. • Comes downstairs backwards on tummy. • Kneels. Bends down to pick things up without falling over when standing. • Carries things around in bags. • Throws balls. • Pulls and pushes large toys about. Pushes small wheeled toys when crawling.	 • Imitates household chores. • Remembers where objects belong. • Recognizes landmarks when out.	• Can fit round and square shapes into holes. • Builds tower of three bricks. • Makes side-to-side marks on paper with crayon. • Turns pages of book, several at a time.
1½-2 years	• Runs • Walks backwards. • Pulls toys on string, first when walking backwards, then forwards. • Walks upstairs with helping hand, two feet to a step. 	• Recognizes familiar faces in photographs. • Can match two identical objects.	• Uses wrist to turn knobs and screw lids. • Works zip. • Starts using one hand in preference to other.
2-2½ years	• Can swerve to avoid obstacles and stop easily when running. • Walks up and down stairs, two feet to a step, with one hand on wall. • Squats on floor to play with toys. • Moves ride-on toy along, using feet against ground. • Kicks football. Throws small ball overarm. • Jumps in air or off a low step, both feet together.	• Begins to sort things into like and unlike. • Has increasing understanding of size.	• Builds tower of six bricks. • Does circular scribble with crayon. • Turns pages of book singly. • Can take sweet wrapper off. • Hammers. • Can drum with two sticks.

**Remember that individual babies are unlikely to reach the stages at the precise ages given above. The ages are averages only.*

Listening and talking	Doing things for self	Suitable toys and activities
 • Understands several words when used in context. • Understands simple instructions. • Gradually increases vocabulary, learning new words at the rate of one to three a month.	• Helps self to toys if within reach. • Picks up trainer cup and drinks without help but usually hands back to adult when finished. • Chews well. • Takes socks and mittens off. • Holds arm out for sleeve and foot for shoe when being dressed.	• Encourage first words (see page 16). • Fetching games (page 17). • Hiding and finding games (page 17). • Sand. • Telephone. 
	• Brings food to mouth on spoon but cannot prevent spoon turning over. • Takes off hat and shoes. Holds up arms when being undressed. Steps out of trousers. • May indicate when nappy is dirty or wet.	• Copying games (see page 17). • Dancing to music (page 38). • Push-along toys. • Balls to throw. • Crayons and paper. • Bricks and other stacking toys (pages 32-33). • Shape sorters (page 32). • Peg people, especially in vehicles. Equipment for imitating and make-believe (pages 30-31).
 • Starts learning new words more rapidly. • Points to parts of body when asked. • Links two words together.	 • Puts cup down after drinking. • Takes arms out of coat. • Helps to wash self. • May ask for potty.	• Pull-along toys. • Ride-on toys. • Things to climb on, bounce on and slide down (see page 25). • Story books. • Jigsaws (lift-out and inset type (page 33). • Playdough (page 29). • Painting (pages 26-27). • Turning and screwing toys (page 33). • Threading toys (page 34). • Musical instruments (page 38).
 • Starts to form simple sentences. • Vocabulary continues to grow. • Different parts of speech, e.g. past tense, added. • Grammar improves. • Knows colours.	 • Sits at table. • Takes off trousers. • Puts on mittens, hat, shoes. • Washes and dries hands. • Uses potty.	• Things to balance on and jump off (page 25). • Football. • Skittles. • Things to match and sort (page 34). • Hammer toys. • Construction toys (page 34). • Putting words together (pages 16-17). 

SOME TOYS TO BUY

Below are just a few examples of types of bought toy that there has not been space to say much about elsewhere in this book. All the toys will not necessarily appeal to every child and they are not essential items of equipment but, in general, they are popular with this age group and have good play value.

Cot gym

These are useful to have across the cot when a baby is at the stage of lying on his back and is starting to reach out to grab things. They consist of a variety of objects to spin and rattle, grip and pull on. Besides helping the baby to realize the connection between his senses of sight, touch and sound, a cot gym helps to develop body awareness. He will feel the weight of his head and body as he tries to pull himself up by the grips and will strengthen his neck, arm, chest and back muscles.

Rattles

As with other toys, the play value of rattles varies, depending on the eyes and mouth as well as hands and ears. Choose rattles that can be held in more than one way, that have moveable parts to encourage the baby to explore them with both hands and that have holes or grooves she can poke her fingers or tongue into.

Activity centre

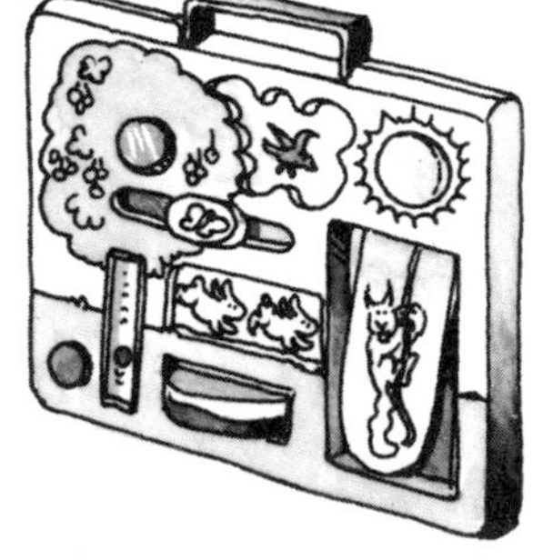

These have a long play life because the manipulative skills they require vary in difficulty, ranging from hitting and pressing to sliding and turning. Each hand action produces a diferent movement and sound, and so encourages understanding of cause and effect. Activity centres based on a theme (house, farm, fairground, for example) also stimulate the imagination and help to develop language skills as you talk about the pictures with the baby.

Ride-on toys

These are excellent for improving a child's co-ordination and balance, as she pushes the toy along with her feet against the ground and learns to steer. They are also fun to climb on and off and generally boost a child's confidence and sense of being in control. Always sit your child on the toy before you buy it to make sure it is the right size. Check, too, that it will not tip over easily and, important for indoor use in most homes, that it can be manoeuvred in a confined space.

Peg people and animals

These are good for developing use of the pincer grip, for shape matching if they can be slotted into vehicles or furniture, for sorting games and, later, for increasingly elaborate games of make-believe.

Steering wheel

The simplest of these attach either to the baby's car seat or buggy and often incorporate a horn. More complex ones, for slightly older children, have a dashboard complete with ignition key, gear stick and indicator levers. They are good for keeping a baby occupied when you cannot give him your full attention such as on car journeys, are an excellent prop for imitative and pretend play and, as the child gets older, may even help to develop rudimentary road sense.

Part 2 – 2½ to 5 years

Robyn Gee

With thanks to: Hilary Abercrombie, Rosalind Barton Zena Barton, Larraine Biscombe, Pam Blackman, Sarah Bokaie, Diane Brending, Sheena Collins, Anne Constable, Janet Cooper, Judith Cross, Lucy Delacombe, Jean Eley, Sue Gross, Janet Gupta, Hilary Hammond, Mavis Midgley, Sally Molson, Wendy Morton, Sharon Mowes, Mandy Parker, Pauline Parker, Irene Pryce, Jill Smith, Gillian Styman, Susan Turner, Janice Whatley, Jackie Wisdom, Hilary Worthington, Valery Wright

Contents of Part 2

In this part of the book you will find lots of ideas to help you entertain young children between the ages of about 2½ and 5 and to help you enjoy the time you spend with them.

The importance of play in the education of young children is now much more widely appreciated than it used to be. Children learn more and at greater speed during the pre-school years than at any other time in their lives. Much research has been done into exactly how and what they learn through play but it is not always obvious to the non-expert how certain types of play contribute to the learning process. The introduction to each topic in this book gives you a brief outline of the learning value of the activities.

Children will play, provided they are not actually prevented from doing so, whether or not they have help from adults but there is no doubt that the learning quality of their play can be greatly influenced by the adults around them. Adults can provide materials, suggest directions, give advice and encouragement and open the door to new activities.

The emphasis in this book is on activities for adults and children to share together.

The selection of activities has been limited to those that require comparatively little preparation or special equipment. The instructions are addressed to adults but the illustrations may fuel children too with ideas. No precise guidelines have been given on the suitable age for each activity, as this depends so much on the individual child but the degree of adult participation will need to vary subtly according to age and ability level. Adults have to strike a delicate balance between helping and interfering. Try to leave as much room as possible for children to discover things for themselves.

There are also suggestions for how to keep children busy while you get on with the many other things you necessarily have to do as a parent.

It is important to remember not to force an activity in an attempt to make a child learn. Play activities should be enjoyable. Follow a child's apparent interests and accept the way she chooses to do things. The process of actively doing something is much more valuable than the result achieved. Remember too to give encouragement and approval.

DRAWING AND COLOURING

Most children progress by the same stages when they are learning to draw but the age at which they reach each stage varies considerably.

By the age of three, a child can usually hold a pencil between his first two fingers and thumb and use it with good control. It is usually clear by now whether he is right- or left-handed. He begins to want to draw, rather than just scribbling, although the finished drawing is unlikely to be recognizable. Children usually start by drawing "people" – heads with limbs and other features coming straight out of the head.

From about four onwards, a child's drawings start to have more detail. People now have heads, legs, arms and fingers, but their bodies are often achieved by shrinking the head and lengthening the legs. A child may decide what to draw before he starts. This is a major step forward from drawing something first and then stating what it is.

From five, pictures containing several different items are produced and there is often an indication of background such as sky. Children can now colour within outlines.

Making marks on paper is the basis of learning to write and gives practice in controlling hand muscles and co-ordinating hand and eye. Drawing and colouring provide opportunities for learning about colours and shapes as well as stimulating children's powers of observation, imagination and communication. They can also give the sense of achievement and self-esteem common to all forms of creativity.

Ideas for cheap paper

★ Rolls of drawer or wall lining paper
★ Back of left-over wallpaper
★ Used envelopes opened out
★ Wrapping paper from parcels
★ Cereal packets cut up
★ Inserts from new shirts
★ Sugar paper – the cheapest paper to buy from art shops.

It is worth asking local offices if they have any scrap paper. Most throw away masses, especially computer paper that has only been used on one side.

Types of pencil and crayon

★ Wax crayons
★ Ordinary crayons
★ Ordinary lead pencils. Teach your child not to suck them.
★ Felt tip pens and magic markers. Buy non-toxic, impermanent ones which will not leave stains on clothes. Teach your child to put the tops back on.
★ Plastic crayons
★ Charcoal

Chalk and blackboards.
Ordinary chalk is very messy so it is best to buy dustless.

You can buy blackboard paint in hardware stores and paint it on to a wall or piece of hardboard to make a blackboard surface.

Magic slates. These have a built-in erasing device. They are usually quite cheap and do not last long but are excellent for journeys, odd moments during outings and when your child is ill in bed.

Stencils and templates. You can buy these or make them quite simply yourself by cutting shapes out of card.

Colouring books. Though these are often criticized on the grounds that they stifle creativity, there is no evidence for this. Used occasionally, they can give a lot of satisfaction and enjoyment to young children. So too can books of dot-to-dot pictures and simple puzzles.

Tracing, carbon and graph paper. These help to ring the changes. Kitchen greaseproof paper can be used as tracing paper. Carbon paper is fun but rather messy. Graph paper can be good for making patterns.

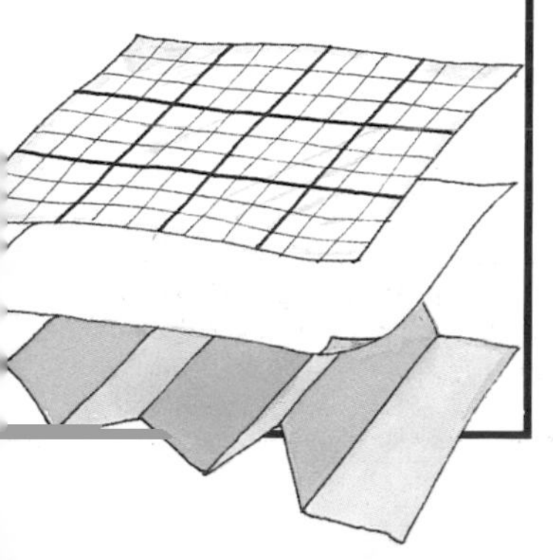

Things to do

Squiggles and swirls. Once your child has grasped the idea of colouring in shapes, try drawing swirly lines all over the paper and letting him colour in the holes.

Outlines. It may help to get an older child started on drawing if you do an outline for him to make into something. If this works, you can turn it into a game and take it in turn to draw outlines for each other, perhaps with your eyes closed.

Hand and foot prints. Try drawing round hands and feet to make an outline. Children enjoy comparing the different sizes of print. Make patterns by covering a sheet of paper with prints and colouring them in.

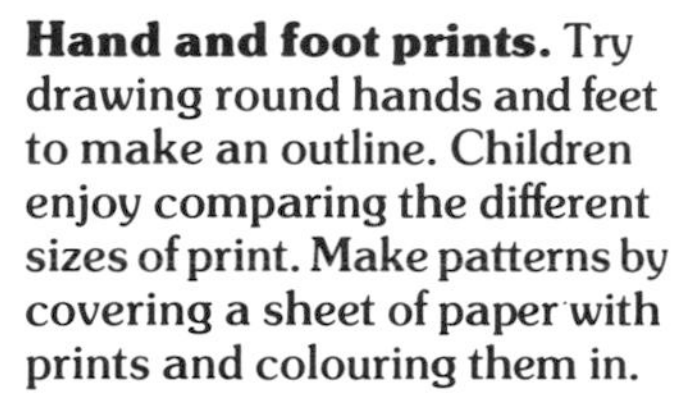

Body prints. If you have a large enough piece of paper (lining paper is ideal) you can get your child to lie down on it and draw his outline. He can then put in features and clothes and colour it in.

Rubbings. Cover objects with thin, plain paper (greaseproof is best) and rub with a wax crayon or soft pencil. Try any firm, textured objects such as coins, keys, patterned floor or wall tiles, shoe soles or bark.

Patterns. Make simple patterns for children to copy, using some of the marks shown here.

PAINTING AND PRINTING

When they first start painting, children need to experiment with the feel of the paint and the way it behaves. Your child may just make a few tentative marks on the painting surface or cover it completely in a single colour. You will have to judge carefully how much help to give. If she is happy with what she is doing, let her carry on. The "doing" is the important part so don't look for results at first.

For a painting session to work, you both need to be relaxed. The same sort of preparations as for the younger age-group (see pages 26-27) are a good idea, so they are re-capped here. It can take half an hour to get everything ready and as long to clear up again so try to ensure your child does not lose interest in painting after only a few minutes by having some suggestions ready. For example, she could start by covering the paper with blobs of colour, then do some stripes before moving on to painting objects such as people or houses.

Materials

Paints. Choose powder paints or liquid poster paints. Paint boxes with hard little blocks of paint are not very satisfactory for young children.

- ★ Poster paint is more convenient, thicker and more expensive than powder paint.
- ★ Powder paint is cheaper, needs mixing with water and is not so thick. You can thicken it by mixing it with wallpaper paste (non-fungicidal), flour and water paste, a PVA glue or soapflakes.

If you mix a little washing up liquid into the paint, it will wash off furniture and clothes more easily.

To start with, two colours of paint, or just one, are enough. Later, if you have red, yellow, blue, white and black, you can mix most other colours from them.

Pots and palettes. You need a pot for each colour of paint and at least one pot for water to wash brushes in. It is also useful to have pots or a surface for mixing different coloured paints together.

Use any container that will not be knocked over too easily. Margarine tubs and large plastic ice cream tubs are good. Yoghurt pots are rather unstable. You can also buy special non-spill paint pots from toyshops.

Old bun tins and plastic egg boxes make good mixing palettes.

Paper. See page 52 for ideas for cheap paper. Many children are quite happy to paint on newspaper to start with.

Brushes. Buy fairly flat ones with short handles. A small decorator's brush works quite well. You could also supply other means of applying paint such as cotton wool swabs or pieces of sponge.

Board or easel. You need some way of holding the paper so it does not move under the brush. The simplest way is to attach it to a piece of hardboard or plywood with tape, bulldog clips or clothes-pegs. Easels are useful but quite expensive to buy.

Protective covering. If you have to worry about where the paint is going, it will take a lot of the fun out of painting sessions, so it is worth providing good protection for clothes, floor and table-tops.

For overalls you can use an old shirt worn back to front with the sleeves cut down; a plastic mac cut down to size; or a carrier bag with the bottom cut out and the handles as shoulder straps.

For table and floor covering use thick layers of newspaper, plastic tablecloths or cheap polythene sheeting bought from a garden centre.

Painting ideas

Finger painting

The easiest way to start a child finger painting is to cover a surface with thick paint and let him draw in it with his fingers.

Old tea trays and plastic-coated boards and worktops make good painting surfaces. If you use paper it has to be fairly thick.

The paint also needs to be thick. You can buy specially thick poster paints called finger paints, or use powder paints or food colouring to colour a thick paste. For the paste use wallpaper glue (non-fungicidal), or flour and water, or one of the recipes below:

1 Mix together ½ cup soapflakes*
½ cup cold water starch
¾ cup cold water

or

2 Dissolve 1 cup cornflour in a little water
Add 1 litre (2 pints) boiling water
Boil until thick
Take off heat
Beat in 1 cup soapflakes*

Some children do not like getting their hands dirty at first. Let your child use something to draw with or try drawing a simple picture and get her to put in dots with her fingers.

Drip painting. Make the paint quite thin and runny. Show your child how to put a blob of paint on the paper and roll it around to make a pattern.

Blow painting. Put blobs of runny paint on the paper and use a straw to blow it into different shapes.

Spray painting. Dip a toothbrush into runny paint and then run your finger over it to send a spray of paint on to the paper. Try making shapes on the paper by placing objects on it before you spray.

Invisible pictures. Use a white candle to draw an invisible picture on a sheet of paper. Then cover the paper with thin paint and the picture will appear.

Rainbows. Use a brush to cover an entire sheet of paper with water, then paint in arches of different colours with a slight gap between them. Watch the arches slowly blend into each other to make a rainbow.

***Make sure you use real soapflakes and not detergent.**

Printing ideas

Children can have a lot of fun experimenting with different ways of printing. This may make fewer demands on the imagination than "free expression" painting but they can get some satisfying results nevertheless. Here are some ideas.

Blob prints. To make blob prints, fold a piece of paper in half, then open it and drop big blobs of runny paint on to one half of the paper near the fold. Fold the clean half over and press hard before opening it up again.

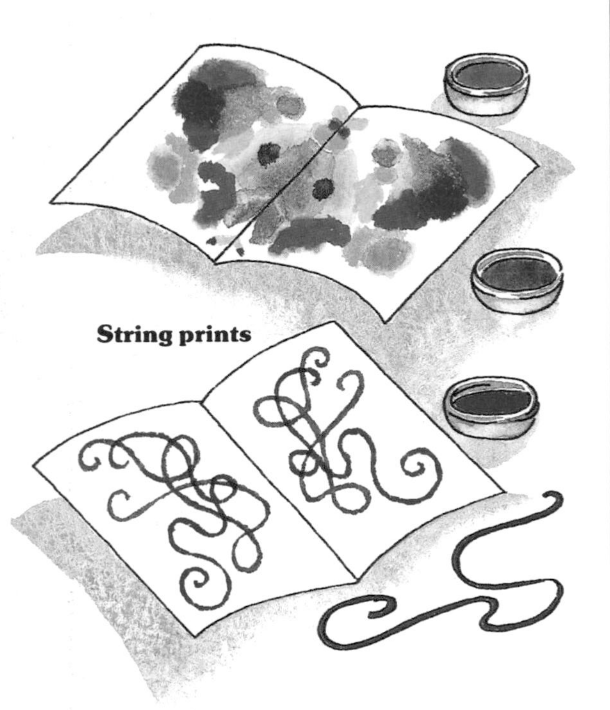

String prints

Dip some string into thickish paint, making sure it gets well covered. Drop it on to one side of a sheet of paper with a fold in it. Fold the other side over and press hard before opening it up.

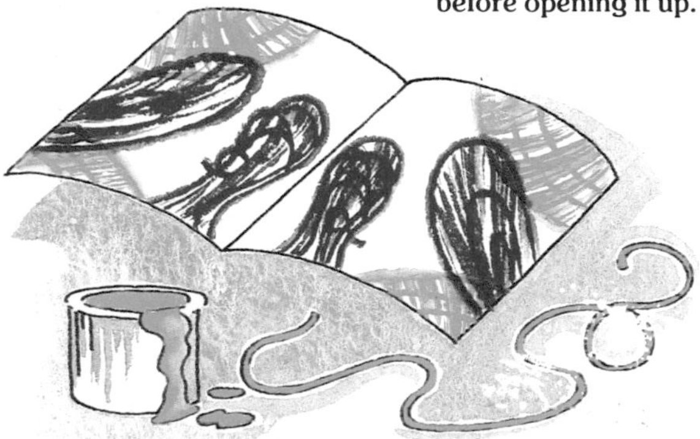

Try leaving one end of the string hanging over the edge of the paper. Then pull the string out while folding and pressing the paper. Repeat with different colours to get the effect above.

Vegetable prints. Various vegetables dipped in paint make interesting prints.

To make potato prints, cut a potato in half and carve shapes in the cut surface.

Hand and foot prints. Put fairly thick paint on to an old tray or unbreakable plate and let your child print in it with different parts of his hands and feet.

Using a screen. Use a paper doily or cut shapes through both thicknesses of a folded piece of paper to make a screen. Place the screen on top of another piece of paper and spread paint over it with a brush or sponge.

You can also try laying the screen over a tray of paint and pressing a clean sheet of paper over the top.

Using blocks. You can make printing blocks quite simply by cutting designs into blocks of plasticine, foam rubber or polystyrene (the type used for packing fragile objects).

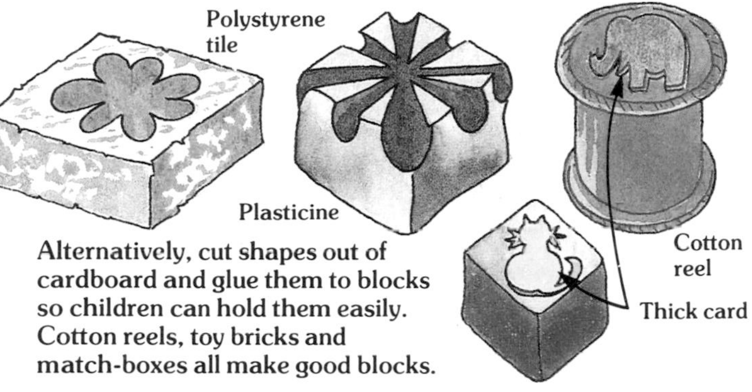

Alternatively, cut shapes out of cardboard and glue them to blocks so children can hold them easily. Cotton reels, toy bricks and match-boxes all make good blocks.

Printed decorations. Make wrapping paper or a poster by printing a design all over a sheet of paper. For parties, print on to tablecloths, napkins, mats, cups and hats made of plain paper.

Printing tips and hints

★ The secret of making good prints is to have the paint the right thickness. You may need to experiment with this, using flour as a thickener and water as a thinner.

★ Thick, non-shiny paper works best. Putting a thick wad of newspaper under the paper helps to get clear prints.

★ Use a brush to put the paint on to the printing object or dip it into the paint. It may be easier to use a piece of thick cloth, sponge or foam rubber.

★ It is handy to have somewhere to dry prints. You could rig up a string drying line and hang them up with clothes-pegs.

★ To make a change, try printing in white and light colours on to black paper.

Other things to try

The choice of objects to print with is almost limitless. Here are just a few suggestions.

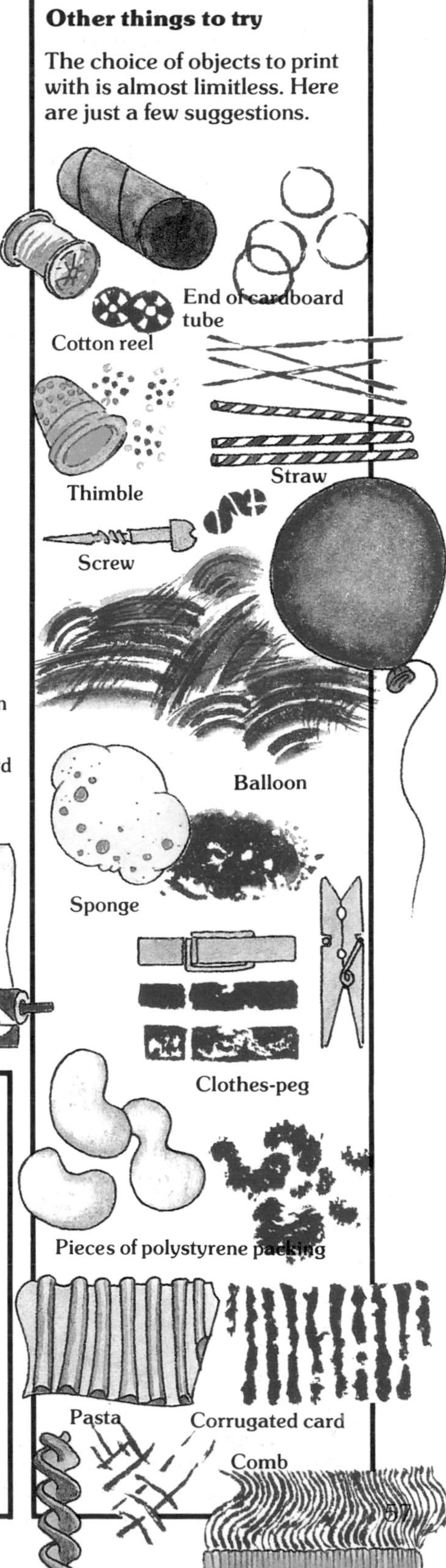

CUTTING AND STICKING

There is a huge range of different materials that can be used for cutting and sticking. As well as developing children's hand control, cutting and sticking stimulates their imagination and creativity, whether they are working out how best to use the materials they have, or are spotting new ones that they could use. It is also a good way of making cards and presents for people.

Learning to use scissors

This is a fairly difficult skill to master and children should always be supervised when using scissors. These should be sharp enough to cut easily but have rounded ends. "Safety" scissors, which have a plastic coating over the blades, are a good idea. They are often made in animal shapes.

Children usually start by holding the scissors in both hands and find straight lines easiest to cut. Try drawing a pencil line on the paper for your child to follow. Then, once she can follow straight lines, start her on curves and circles. Old newspaper is useful for practising on.

If your child has difficulty in using scissors, there are lots of things she can make by tearing paper instead of cutting.

Types of glue

Be careful when choosing glue. Never give your child a glue which gives off vapours and don't use glues which say they give "instant bonding".

★ Liquid glues are quite adequate for sticking paper to paper.
★ Glue sticks are also good for gluing paper to paper and for other lightweight materials.
★ PVA (polyvinyl acetate) glue is strong and good for sticking heavier materials. It is white but goes transparent when dry.
★ Flour and water paste can be used if you have no proper glue. Mix together flour and water to make a smooth paste. Bring to the boil and simmer for a few moments.
★ Wallpaper paste is good for sticking paper, but be sure to use a non-fungicidal type.

Things to cut and stick

All the things listed below could come in useful but you will only need a small selection at a time, say up to six things.

Paper and card
Old newspapers
Tissue paper
Crêpe paper
Scraps of wallpaper
Used wrapping paper
Old birthday and Christmas cards
Old magazines
Old catalogues and leaflets
Gummed paper
Gummed paper shapes
Thick paper or card (for the base for collage pictures)

Things from the kitchen
Kitchen foil
Drinking straws
Doilies
Seeds (melon, marrow, sunflower, for example)
Egg shells (wash and leave to dry, then crush.)
Egg boxes
Foil tops and wrappers
Pasta
Lentils
Beans
Rice
Cereal
Salt
Spices
Herbs
Tea
Coffee
Cocoa

Miscellaneous
Cotton wool
Glitter (Use with care.)

Sewing materials
Wool
Embroidery silk
Ribbon
Scraps of fabric

Things from out-of-doors
Twigs
Feathers
Small shells
Pressed flowers and grasses
Wood-shavings
Sawdust
Sand (Light-coloured sand can be coloured. Put a little dry sand into an old jam jar, add a few drops of food colouring and shake well. Then spread the sand on a sheet of paper to dry.)

Ideas for things to make

Dancing dolls. Make several concertina-style folds in a piece of paper. Cut out a figure with arms outstretched to the edges of the paper. Unfold and you have a row of people.

Paper snowflakes. Cut a circle out of thin white paper and fold it in half three times. Snip little pieces from the sides and open out.

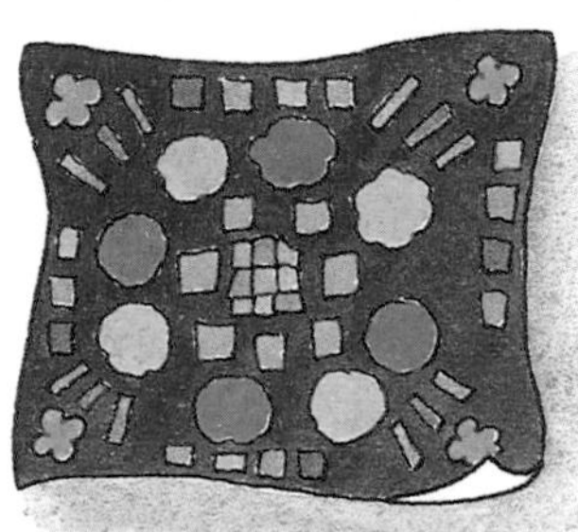

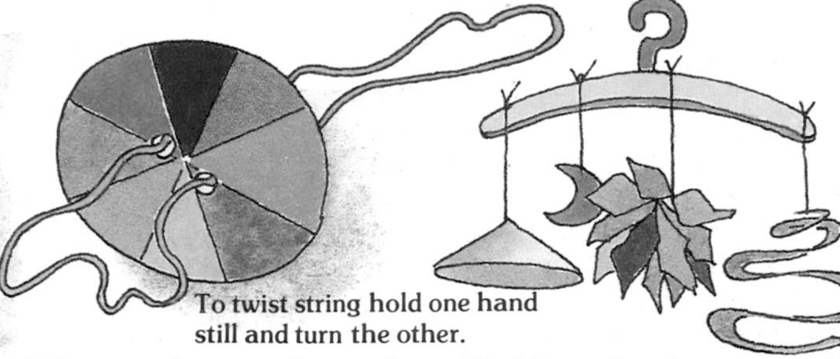

Mosaics. Tear or cut coloured paper or pictures from magazines into small bits. Stick them on a piece of paper to make a mosaic, or as decoration on boxes or tins.

Whizzer. Cut a circle out of card and colour it in several colours. Make two holes in the centre, thread string through and tie it. Twist the string, then pull outwards to make the circle whizz round.

Mobiles. Cut shapes out of coloured card, tie or stick them to pieces of thread and hang them from a coat-hanger to move gently in a draught.

Fish collage. Draw or cut out the shape of a fish and glue on silver milk bottle tops to give the effect of scales. Strips of blue and green tissue paper make a good sea background.

Princess collage. Draw or cut out a princess with a large ball gown. Decorate the gown with scraps of material, tissue paper or foil.

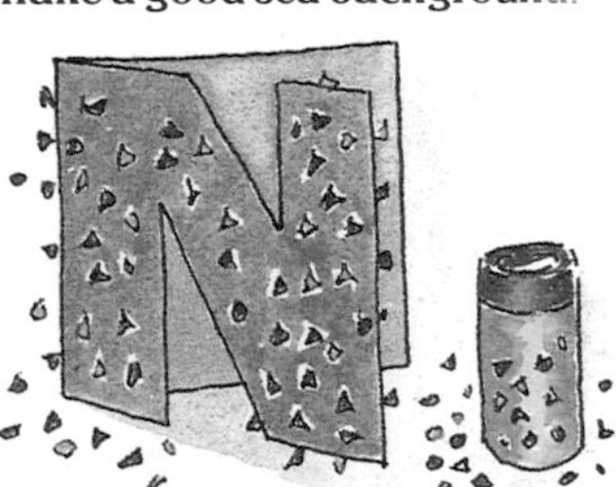

Cut-out cards. Make cards for friends by folding paper in half and cutting out the initial letter of their name or their age.

Pop-up cards. Fold a piece of paper in half and cut out a shape, then glue it by its edges across the centre of a card.

Other collage ideas
Ideas for collage are limitless. Here are a few more suggestions:

Tissue paper vase of flowers
Drinking straw hedgehog
Egg-shell tortoise
Egg-box monster
Fluffy chicken (use yellow cotton wool)
Stained glass window (use cellophane or tissue paper)
Night-time scene (use silver foil on black background)

You could also try copying a simple picture from a book, or doing a portrait of a teddy, favourite animal or member of the family.

MODELLING AND BUILDING

Modelling and building give children the opportunity to learn about different materials and the way they behave. It is both a tactile and a creative activity, giving scope to the imagination and building self-confidence. It can even be the first step towards learning to appreciate the visual arts such as sculpture. On a more commonplace level, it is soothing and relaxing.

Making playdough

You can buy playdough but it is quite simple to make. The recipe below for long-lasting playdough has already been given on page 29, but here you will find ideas for variations, too.

Basic playdough. Flour and water are the basic ingredients. Salt helps to preserve it and keep it moist, but makes it a little brittle. Oil helps to counteract this, making it glossy and pliable. You need approximately two measures of flour for every one of salt and water.

2 cups plain flour
1 cup salt
1 cup cold water
1 tablespoon oil

Adding colour. Use food colouring or paint. For a smooth, even colour, mix the colouring with the water before it is added to the flour and salt; for a streaky, marbled effect, knead it straight into the dough.

Adding smells. To ring the changes try adding one of the following: peppermint essence, ginger, cinnamon or rosewater. Don't do this for smaller children as it may increase the temptation to eat the dough.

Stretchy playdough. Instead of plain flour mix self-raising flour with water to make a dough that is puffy and stretchy but does not last very long.

Long-lasting playdough. By adding cream of tartar to the recipe and cooking the mixture you can make a dough that lasts well and has a lovely texture.

2 teaspoons cream of tartar
1 cup plain flour
½ cup salt
1 tablespoon oil
1 cup water

Mix to form a smooth paste. Put in a saucepan and cook slowly, until the dough comes away from the side of the pan and forms a ball. When it is cool enough, take the dough out of the pan and knead for three to four minutes. Put the pan to soak immediately.

Making things from junk

Collecting junk. Start by collecting boxes (cereal and tea packets, shoe boxes, match-boxes, juice containers), tubes (paper towel and toilet roll, washing up liquid bottles, herb pots) and tubs (margarine, ice-cream and yoghurt cartons). You will soon develop an eye for other things that will come in handy.

Building blocks. Stuff the boxes, tubes and tubs with newspaper and tape the ends closed. To paint them mix up some powder paints and add a little washing up liquid to make the paint spread more easily.

Fixing and sticking. The following can all be used to help to construct things from boxes, tubes and tubs: ordinary paper clips, split-pin paper clips, hair grips, rubber bands, staples, sticky tape, pieces of string, pipe cleaners, PVA glue. Here are some things you could make.

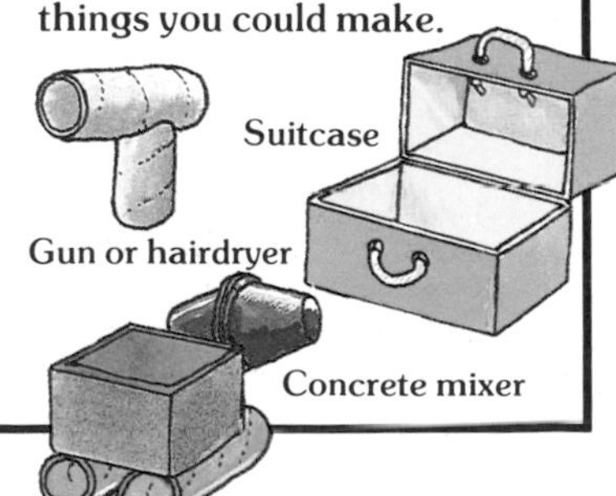

Playing with playdough

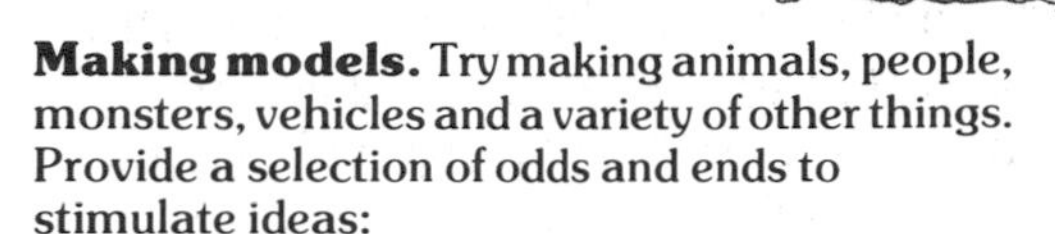

This is not necessarily a messy activity, but don't play over a carpet or rug as bits can easily get trodden in. Formica, plastic tablecloths or large trays make the best work surfaces.

Squeezing, pinching and punching. When they are first introduced to playdough, children are often happy simply to handle it and squash it about, without trying to make anything. Let them explore its possibilities by themselves for a while.

Play cooking. It is very useful to have some playdough handy for when you want to cook without children joining in. Provide some implements so that they can imitate what they see:

Rolling pin (You can make one out of a small piece of dowelling or broom handle.)
Shape cutters
Plastic knives
Spatula
Variety of containers and their lids (to act as bowls, plates and pans)

Making models. Try making animals, people, monsters, vehicles and a variety of other things. Provide a selection of odds and ends to stimulate ideas:

Pebbles	Bottle caps
Used matches	Buttons
Drinking straws (cut into pieces)	Wool
	String
Lolly sticks	Rubbish bag ties

Sculpting. Let a lump of playdough go a bit dry and carve it with plastic knives or used matches.

Making things to keep. To make models last, bake them in a fairly hot oven until they go hard (about 10 to 20 minutes depending on size). When cool they can be painted with poster paints.

Try making pretend food for dolls and teddies, play money for shops, and jewellery for dressing up (see page 77).

Storing playdough

Playdough dries out when exposed to air so if you want it to last, store it in an airtight container, such as a plastic bag or box, and keep it in the fridge. Kept like this, the basic playdough will last for a week or two and the long-lasting dough for several months. If it gets left out accidentally and starts going dry and crumbly, you may be able to rescue it with a little water and oil.

Woodwork

Children can get a lot out of working with real tools and wood at a surprisingly early age. You need to supervise them carefully and show them how to use each tool properly.

Hammer, nails and wood. Hammering nails into wood can be very absorbing. Strength and aim are not good at first, so provide a strong, light hammer, nails with large heads and soft wood.

Glue and paint. To stick pieces of wood together, use PVA glue. To paint, use powder or poster paint with some PVA glue mixed in.

Saws and clamps. Some four and five-year-olds can use saws very competently. A saw needs to be strong and sharp – a tenon or junior hacksaw is best. The wood must be held in a vice or G-clamp.

Screws and screwdrivers. Use a gimlet, bradawl or drill to make holes in a piece of wood. The child can then practise screwing in screws.

Sandpaper, files and planes. Some children really enjoy simply working on a piece of wood to make it smooth.

BOOKS, PICTURES AND STORIES

It is never too early to introduce your child to books, both for the enjoyment they provide and for their learning value. Looking at books together is also a valuable shared experience which can strengthen the emotional links between you. Use books as often as possible but never force them on a child who would clearly prefer to be doing something else.

Using books helps to develop children's powers of observation and their ability to listen. It improves their skill at talking and encourages the desire to communicate. Use of language is closely linked with the ability to think. Books also stimulate the imagination and encourage emotional development as the child begins to appreciate how other people feel. They extend his knowledge of the world by introducing him to new situations and deepening his understanding of those he has already experienced.

If a child is used to books and enjoys them, he is more likely to want to learn to read. Looking at books early teaches him valuable pre-reading skills, such as an awareness of detail and the knack of moving his eyes from left to right.

A child's attitude to books is conditioned by his parents'. If he sees that you enjoy reading and refer to books for information he is likely to think of books as enjoyable.

Choosing and using books

Which books? Introduce your child to as great a variety as possible: books with different types of illustration, some detailed, some simple, for example; books with different subject matter such as stories, information or rhymes; books of different size, shape and length. Be guided by your own taste and your child's enthusiasms. Some books will be mainly for looking at and talking about; others will be for reading.

Libraries. Borrowing books from the library is the best way of providing your child with variety and allowing him to develop his taste without any expense. There is usually a children's librarian who can advise you which books to choose. Many libraries organize story-telling sessions to encourage children's interest in books.

Bookshops. Try to find a bookshop that encourages browsing, can give you advice and has facilities for children, such as a special reading corner. Second-hand bookshops and jumble sales can be good places for buying picture books cheaply.

Book clubs and book parties. Book clubs sell books at reduced prices, usually in return for a promise that you will buy a certain number of books a year. They send you information about current offers, including the age range each book is suitable for, and you order by post.

Book parties are held in people's homes and provide a good opportunity to look at books and discuss them with others before you buy them.

Storytime. It is a good idea to have a certain time each day that is specially devoted to books, perhaps just before bedtime. The attention you give your child, the physical closeness, warmth and feeling of security will all contribute to his enjoyment of books.

Reading aloud. If you start by talking through picture books with your child, reading stories will follow naturally. Always read slowly and clearly, and try to change expression and pace to hold his interest. You can alter or shorten the text if you think it is too hard but remember that stories are a good opportunity for children to learn new words.

Fathers and reading. It is important for fathers to make a special effort to read and to be seen reading. Far more boys than girls are poor readers. The reason for this is thought to be that most teachers of young children are female and mothers read to their children more than fathers, so boys can get the impression that men do not care about books.

Book corners. It is a good idea to have a small, cosy corner somewhere in the house that is specially for books. This will encourage your child to look at books by himself.

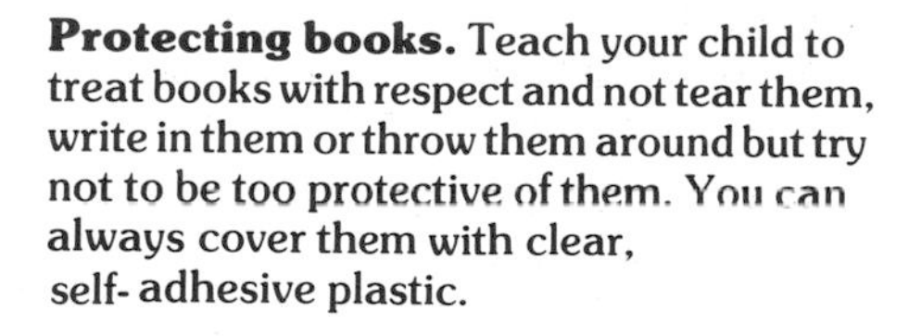

Protecting books. Teach your child to treat books with respect and not tear them, write in them or throw them around but try not to be too protective of them. You can always cover them with clear, self- adhesive plastic.

Books and television. Don't make books compete with television for your child's attention by having the television on in the background while you are reading together. Children who otherwise show little interest in books may start to enjoy them by looking at books based on their favourite programmes. Don't let television become a substitute for books.

Making your own books

Helping your child to make his own book is a good way of encouraging a liking for books.

Buy a scrapbook or notebook, or fold large sheets of paper in half, punch two holes along the fold and thread string, wool or ribbon through them.

A book about me. Include drawings or photographs of family, friends, pets, toys, bedroom, favourite things, holidays, birthday, favourite foods.

Favourite topics. Collect pictures from old magazines on favourite topics such as cars, animals or food.

Shape and colours. Collect pictures of different shaped objects and have a page for each shape. Do the same for colours.

Stories. If your child is starting to show an interest in writing, help him to make up a story and write down what he dictates. He can then illustrate the story.

Making up stories

You do not need a special talent or brilliant imagination to make up stories that your child will enjoy. A photograph or picture may help to start you off. You can even get your child's assistance by asking "What do you think happened next?" and building his answers into the story.

Most children love thinly disguised stories about themselves and also like stories about what their parents did when they were small. The tiniest incidents soon get elaborated on and become favourite family tales.

If you turn a story into a serial to give you time to make up the next episode, remember always to leave it at an exciting part.

FUN WITH WORDS AND LETTERS

a w

Playing games which involve recognizing letters of the alphabet and whole words is something most small children will enjoy if it is approached in the right way. It can also form the basis of learning to read and write. It is unwise, though, to place too much emphasis on the "learning to read" aspect of the games. If this starts to override the play element, it can do more harm than good.

When are children ready for these games?

They are ready when they show an interest if you point out words and letters on signs and in books, or write things for them. Seeing their own name written down usually interests them at this stage and the first letter of their name is usually the first they recognize. They will be more interested if they enjoy being read to and have some understanding of the usefulness of reading. They must have a well-developed awareness of detail to be able to distinguish the differences between letter shapes. Their concentration and memory must also be sufficiently developed. These skills of memory, concentration and visual awareness form an important part of what are often termed the "pre-reading skills".

Capital letters and small letters

Many capital letters bear little relation in shape to their small (lower case) equivalents, so learning both sets is almost like learning two alphabets. To make it easier, children are usually taught only small letters to start with. However, use capitals where common sense suggests it, such as for the first letters of names.

Letter sounds and letter names

Most experts feel it is better to tell children the letter sounds rather than the letter names – "kuh" rather than "see" for "c" – as it makes it easier for them to join the letters up into words later on. However, letters sounded in isolation sound very different from the way they are pronounced in a word and it is debatable whether it makes a great deal of difference.

Teaching methods and reading schemes

Parents often worry that starting to teach their children to read may actually confuse them when they go to school. This only happens in rare cases where a school sticks very rigidly to an unusual reading method.

The "phonic" method involves recognizing letters and letter sounds and building up words from them. The "look and say" method involves learning to recognize whole words and so having the satisfaction of being able to read sentences earlier. Most schools use a combination of these methods and it is best to play games that involve recognition of whole words as well as single letters.

How to form the letters of the alphabet

It is important when writing letters for children, or teaching them how to write, that you know how to form each letter correctly yourself. This is shown below.

a b c d e f g h i j k l m n

o p q r s t u v w x y z

Learning to recognize words

A word's overall shape is composed of its length and the arrangement of the letters' up and down "tails" (ascenders and descenders). It is as easy to learn to recognize whole word shapes as it is to recognize words from their individual letters, although initial letters may provide a clue to what the word is.

Word cards

These are pieces of card, usually about the size of a postcard, with one word written on each. They are used to help children learn to recognize words and are very simple to make. It is best if you start with your child's name and then move on to people and things she knows well. Introduce the cards one at a time, waiting until she knows each word before going on to the next. Once she can recognize several cards, there are all sorts of games you can play – below are some ideas. You could also make picture cards to match each word card.

Snap. Write each word on several cards. You can also add pictures to make it easier. Each have a pile and take it in turns to turn over a card. First one to spot a pair shouts "Snap".

Find the pair. Use pairs of words or words and pictures. Start by having the cards turned face up to look for pairs. Move on to having them all face down except one and take it in turns to turn over a card until you find its pair. Then take it in turns to turn over two cards at once, aiming to find a matching pair.

Word bingo. Have large cards divided into squares. Write a word, or stick or draw a picture, in each square. Take it in turns to pick up a word card. If it matches a word or picture on your large card, place it on top of it. The first to cover a complete row or, if you prefer, the whole card, is the winner.

Action cards. Write an action word such as "jump", "sit", "run" on each card. The game involves picking out a card and doing the action written on it as quickly as possible. You could also write the names of pieces of furniture that have to be touched or rooms that have to be visited.

Recognizing letter sounds

It takes a lot of practice for children to be able to recognize letter sounds when they form part of a word. Once your child can recognize one or two letter sounds at the beginning of words, you can try some games.

I spy. "I spy with my little eye something beginning with –." Give additional clues to start with, for example: "It's black, it purrs and it begins with 'kuh'."

Odd one out. Say a number of words, all but one of which begin with the same letter, and see if your child can spot the odd one out. If he gets good at this, try it with last letters.

Rhymes. Playing around with rhymes helps a great deal with recognition of similar sounds. Play rhyming versions of I spy and Odd man out, for example: "Can you see something that rhymes with 'bat'?"

Alphabet scrapbook. Write a letter at the top of each page of a scrapbook. Concentrating on a few letters at a time, collect pictures of objects that begin with those letters and stick them on the appropriate pages. Write the names of the objects underneath.

Learning to write letters

The manual skill needed to write words develops more slowly than the ability to read them.

Pencils should be held lightly between the thumb and first two fingers about 3cm from the point.

Left-handers should grip even further from the point so that they can see what they are writing. Their paper should be slightly to the left of centre of their bodies and either parallel to the edge of the table or slanted slightly to the right.

Recognizing letter shapes

As well as the 26 small letters, there are 17 new capital letter shapes to be learnt. Over half the letters of the alphabet can become other letters if they are turned over or twisted round and children often find this confusing. Here are some games to help them.

Letter cards. You can use letter cards in the same way as word cards (see page 73). Introduce the letters one at a time, in whatever order you find easiest, but avoid introducing letters of similar shape too close together. Wait until your child knows each new shape before introducing the next one.

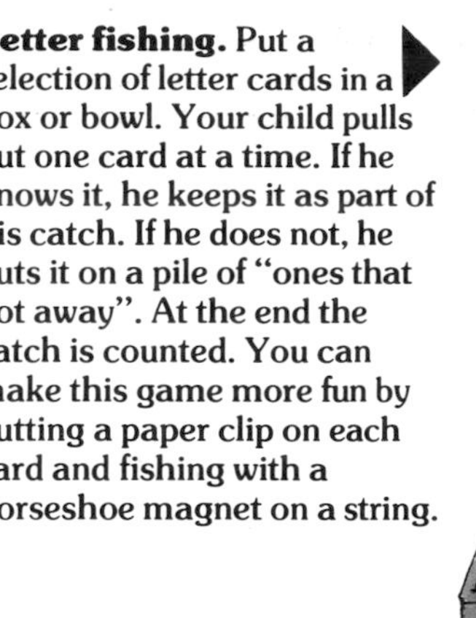

Letter fishing. Put a selection of letter cards in a box or bowl. Your child pulls out one card at a time. If he knows it, he keeps it as part of his catch. If he does not, he puts it on a pile of "ones that got away". At the end the catch is counted. You can make this game more fun by putting a paper clip on each card and fishing with a horseshoe magnet on a string.

Letter building. Cut out a selection of shapes – short, medium and long straight pieces, half circles, hooks and arches. You can play around with these together to see what letters you can make. Give your child a selection of two or three shapes and ask him what letters he can make out of them. You can also have fun making letters out of pipe-cleaners and playdough.

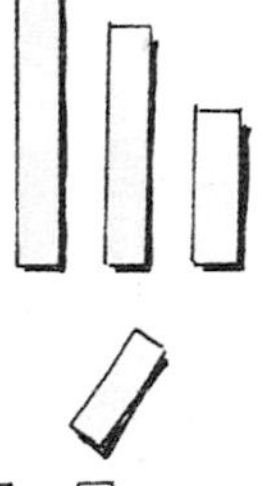

Post a letter. Cut a slot in an empty cereal packet or shoe box. Ask your child if she can find an "m" to send to a monkey, or a "p" to send to a pig and so on with other letters of the alphabet.

Patterns. The formation of letters is based on certain recurring patterns. Copying patterns helps to increase manual control and prepare the way for writing.

Sand or salt tray. Children enjoy writing with their fingers and have more control that way than when using pencils and pens. Writing letters with finger paints is also fun.

Tracing and joining up dotted letters. This is useful because it helps to imprint on a child's mind the feel of writing letters without his having to think too hard about how to form them.

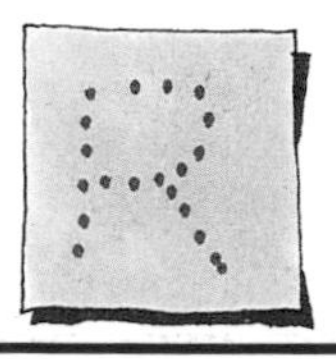

Fill in the first letter. Filling in a letter to complete a word is a useful first step towards writing a whole word.

FUN WITH NUMBERS

Numbers, like letters, can provide a lot of entertainment for small children. They first become familiar with the sound of numbers, then begin to understand the concept of them and to recognize them when they are written down. Learning to count requires a great deal of repetition and games are the best way to make the repetition interesting.

Many other activities contribute considerably to mathematical skill later in life. Number play is just a part of this. Matching, sorting and ordering, playing with shapes, and other activities which develop the concepts of position, size and amount are all important too.

The sound of numbers

Children can start to recognize the sound of numbers from a very early age if they hear number songs and rhymes and hear people counting. They may even appear to be able to count by reciting numbers from one to ten but this has very little meaning for them. They then start to notice numbers in everyday speech and to develop some understanding of the context in which they are used.

Numbers all around

Point out numbers that appear in different everyday contexts. This helps children to begin not only to recognize written numbers but to understand that they have a practical use, helping to distinguish one thing or amount from another.

Learning to count

Before learning to count properly, a child needs to understand what teachers refer to as "one-to-one correspondence". This simply means being able to match one object to one other object or person.

You can practise this in all sorts of different contexts, counting the objects once your child starts to get the idea. Laying the table is a good one. Drawing is another.

As you count objects together, touch each one. Don't start by trying to count objects that you cannot touch. Touching helps children to understand that they are counting one thing at a time.

Don't go beyond three until your child has really mastered counting up to three. Then add one more number at a time.

Occasionally mix up the order of the things you are counting to make sure your child does not think a certain object has a certain number.

Things to do

Counting trays. Use an egg carton, a bun tin or a collection of plastic tubs. Write numbers on the bottom of the containers or on bits of paper to put into them. Provide a pile of dried beans or pasta and show your child how to count the appropriate number into each container. Underline 6 and 9 to avoid confusion.

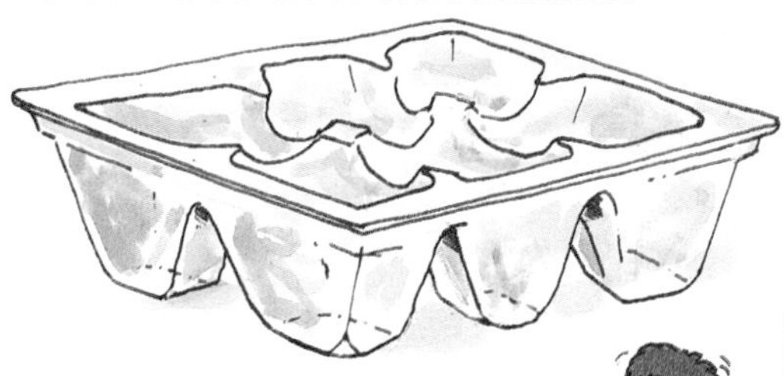

Step, hop, jump. Take it in turns to give instructions to each other, such as "Take three big steps, two tiny hops and one jump". When the player makes a mistake, it is her turn to give instructions to you.

Throwing games. Games which involve throwing a number of objects into a container, such as a waste paper basket, can give good counting practice.

Dice games. You can make games to play with dice quite easily by drawing a course, like the one below, on a piece of paper. Choose objects to move round the course. The dice determines the moves each player makes.

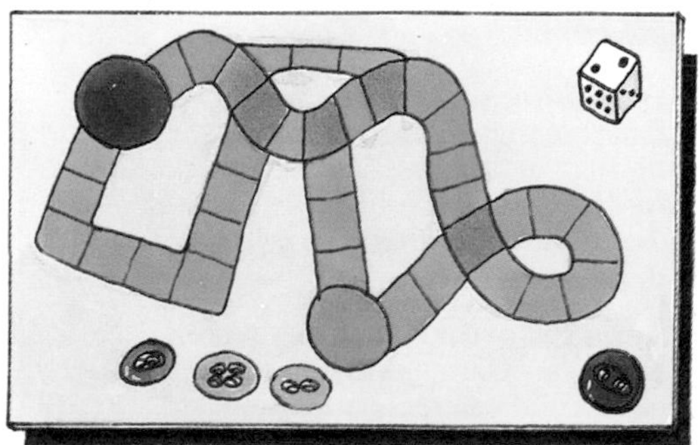

Number cards. Make number cards from pieces of card about the size of large postcards. On one side of each card write a number and on the other draw and colour in the corresponding number of large spots. Some people cut shapes out of gummed paper and stick them on instead. Others sew buttons on.

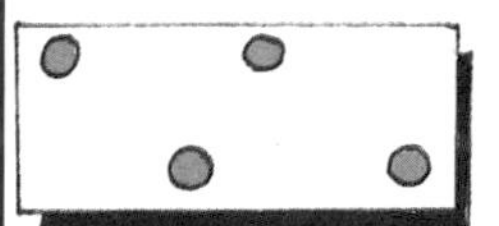

Lay the cards out, spotted sides up. Ask your child to put them in order or leave one out and see if she can tell which one is missing.

Try making two or more cards for each number but arrange the spots differently on each one. See if your child can match the cards with the same number of spots.

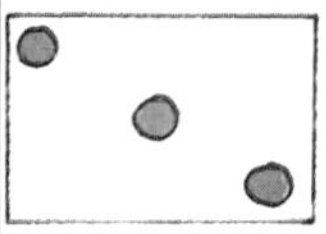

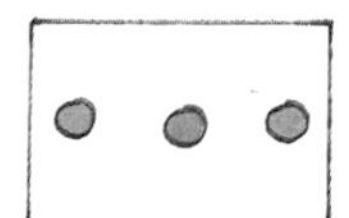

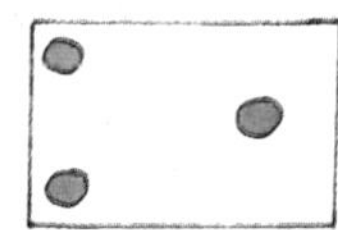

Give your child a pile of counters, buttons or coins. Show her the number written on one card. She then has to give you that number of counters. She can check her answer by placing them on top of the spots on the other side of the card.

Make bingo cards by dividing large sheets of paper into rectangles the same size as your number cards. Write a number in each rectangle. Each person takes a card and if its number appears on their bingo sheet uses it to cover the number up. Continue until someone fills their sheet and shouts "Bingo".

Shopping games. A play shop gives excellent opportunities for counting out money and, later, for adding up different amounts and subtracting to find the right change. Write prices on the goods for sale.

LISTENING TO AND MAKING MUSIC

Parents can introduce their children to music in two main ways. First, by making them aware of sound and helping them to learn to listen. Listening is an acquired art that children develop through practice. It is worth helping to develop this skill because it plays such an important part in learning and communication in general and not just in musical activities. Second, they can encourage them to experiment with making sound and using their bodies to respond to it.

You do not need to have musical ability or any knowledge of music to be able to help your child develop an interest in and enjoyment of music. While it is true that musical ability is a natural gift, nearly everyone is capable of getting a great deal out of music, provided they are exposed to it in ways that they enjoy.

Apart from straightforward enjoyment, music can bring other benefits. Children who have learnt to listen to songs, and join in, tend to become more confident in their use of words – speech therapists use musical activities specifically to help children with speech defects. It is also an excellent vehicle for releasing tension and letting off steam.

Choosing music to listen to

Provide plenty of variety in your choice of music for your child to listen to and avoid trying to impose your own musical tastes. Children have a very short attention span when just listening, so choose short pieces. Follow what you know a child enjoys and watch for signs that a piece has caught their attention, however briefly.

Most children prefer music with strong rhythms which suggest movement; band music tends to go down well. If there are words they need to be very clear for a child to understand them when sung. Point out the sounds of individual instruments if they are easy to pick out.

Learning to listen

The first stage in learning to listen is to become aware of as many different sounds as possible. You can encourage this in a variety of ways. Simply pointing out sounds and talking about them is very helpful and provides children with words with which to describe sound. Below is a selection of games which encourage listening.*

Listening games

How many sounds? Get children to close eyes, keep still and count the number of sounds they can hear. Works best outside.

What am I doing now? One person closes eyes, the other has to guess what they are doing – things like opening a door, bouncing a ball, turning the pages of a newspaper.

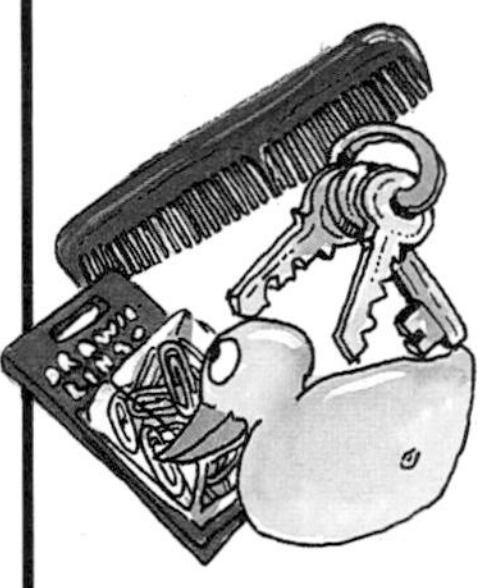

What made the noise? Select three or four objects that make different noises. Listen to the noises. Child closes eyes while you remove one, and then has to work out which one is missing.

Paper sounds. Listen together to the different sounds made by tearing, crumpling or flapping paper. Child has to close eyes and guess which you are doing. Try also using different types of paper – tissue, wrapping, newspaper. Child has to guess which you are using.

Dropping sounds. Choose three different things, such as a coin, a paper clip and a pencil, to drop into a box or tin. Child has to close eyes and guess which is being dropped. Try also using a selection of different containers.

Tape recorded sounds. Record a selection of familiar sounds and voices and see if child can recognize them.

**See page 7 for how to develop listening skills in babies.*

Singing and dancing

Children's first experience of making music usually comes when they join in songs or tunes with actions such as clapping, stamping, marching and jumping or by saying odd words they can remember. At first it comes as naturally to them to respond with movement as with sound, but they may become more inhibited about moving to music a little later on.

They learn to join in songs by hearing them constantly repeated. At first they often come in on the last word of a line and this gradually gives them the confidence to do more and more. Strong rhythm and rhyme help them to join in.

If a song has actions to go with it, remember that it is hard for small children to do the actions as well as singing, unless they know the song very well.

Below and on the next page are some popular action songs in case you cannot remember any.* Don't worry if you do not know the tunes. Just choose any tune that seems to work, or make one up as you go along.

Action songs

If you're happy and you know it,
Clap your hands. (Clap, clap)
If you're happy and you know it,
Clap your hands. (Clap, clap)
If you're happy and you know it,
And you really want to show it,
If you're happy and you know it,
Clap your hands. (Clap, clap)

Other verses:
Shake your head
Touch your nose
Jump up and down
Stamp your feet

Wind the bobbin up, (Roll fists round in a
Wind the bobbin up, circle over each other.)
Pull, pull, (Pull fists outwards)
Clap, clap, clap. (Follow actions.)
Point to the ceiling,
Point to the floor,
Point to the window,
Point to the door.
Clap your hands together,
One, two three,
Put your hands upon your knee.

The wheels on the bus go round and round,
Round and round, round and round, (Move hands round in a circle.)
The wheels on the bus go round and round,
All day long.

Other verses:

The wipers on the bus go swish, swish, swish (Move forearms from side to side.)

The people on the bus go up and down (Stand up, sit down.)
The horn on the bus goes peep, peep, peep (Press horn while peeping.)

Oh, the Grand Old Duke of York, (March on the spot.)
He had ten thousand men,
He marched them up to the top of the hill, (March forwards.)
And he marched them down again. (March backwards.)

And when they were up they were up, (March forwards.)
And when they were down they were down, (March backwards.)
And when they were only half way up, (One step forwards and
They were neither up nor down. one step backwards.)

**There are more action rhymes on pages 39-41.*

Head and shoulders, knees and toes,
Knees and toes.
Head and shoulders, knees and toes,
Knees and toes.
And eyes and ears and mouth and nose,
Head and shoulders, knees and toes,
Knees and toes.

Other verses: Touch head and shoulders but leave out the words for them. In the next verse leave out the words "Knees and toes". In the next one "eyes and ears" and finally "mouth and nose". After this silent verse sing the whole thing through loudly.

Here we go round the mulberry bush,
The mulberry bush, the mulberry bush,
Here we go round the mulberry bush,
On a cold and frosty morning.

This is the way we wash our hands,
Wash our hands, wash our hands.
This is the way we wash our hands,
On a cold and frosty morning.

Other verses: This is the way we brush our hair, clean our teeth, wave goodbye.

Oh, we can play on the big brass drum,
And this is the music to it:
Boom, boom, boom goes the big brass drum,
And that's the way we do it.

Other verses: tambourine (jingle, jingle, jangle), castanets (click, click, clack)

Making up songs together

Start by playing around with a word that you know your child likes. Say it in lots of different ways – fast, slow, high, low. Develop a rhythm with it and then say something about it.

Build up a song by using lots of repetition with the occasional new statement. Don't worry about making rhymes unless they come very easily to you.

Say the words over and over again and then try singing them. It doesn't matter what it sounds like. Your child will still enjoy it even if you think you cannot sing a note.

When children first start to sing, they sing all on one note. Then they learn that their voices will go high and low and start to control them.

Some ideas for instruments to make

It is usually best to stick to percussion instruments with children under five. If you start by improvising them or making them at home, you will find out what goes down well. When you feel you have exhausted home-made possibilities you can find a wide range of very good children's percussion instruments in good toyshops.

Shakers

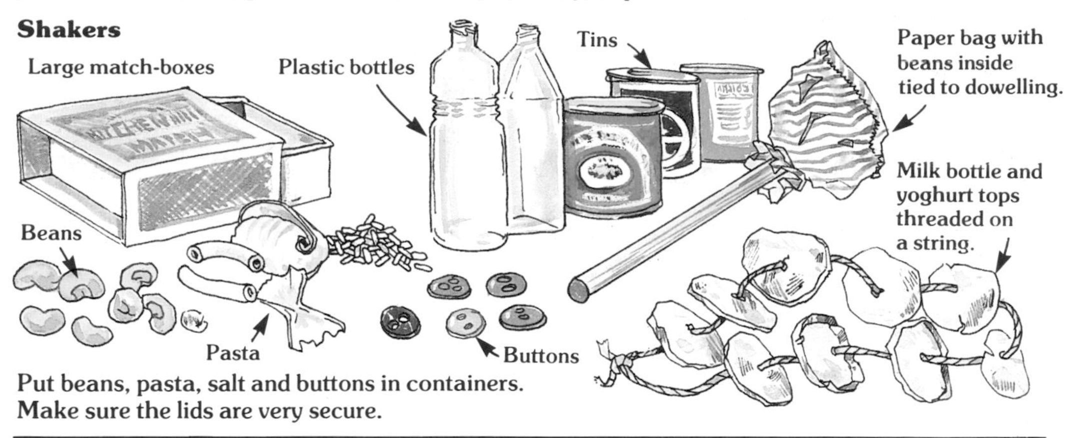

Put beans, pasta, salt and buttons in containers. Make sure the lids are very secure.

Drums

Any of these containers hit with a wooden or metal spoon makes a good drum. You can also make drum heads by tying greaseproof paper over them.

Chimes

Hang metal objects on lengths of wool and hit with metal spoons.

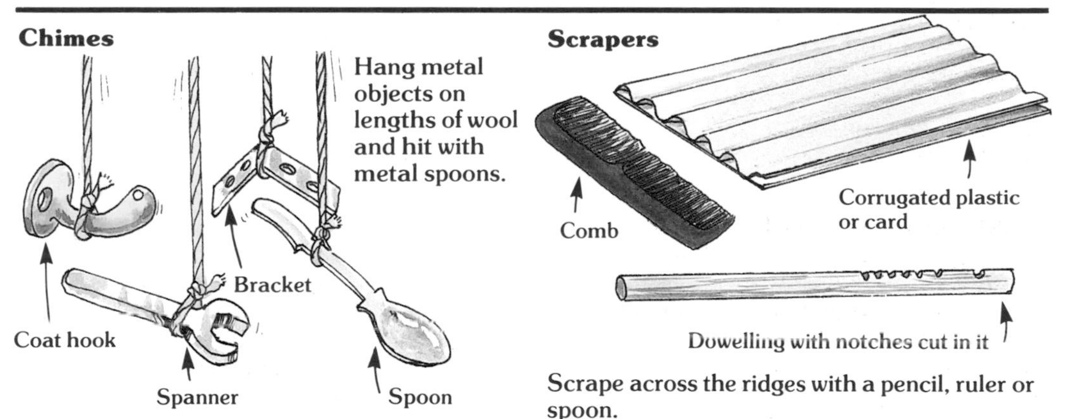

Scrapers

Scrape across the ridges with a pencil, ruler or spoon.

Learning to play an instrument

Most children do not start learning an instrument with a teacher until they are at least seven. A notable exception to this is the Suzuki method of learning the violin, piano or cello, in which children can start at about three. They do not learn from written music, but by imitation, through listening to records and playing games. Practice is done frequently but in small doses. The method undoubtedly works but requires the intimate involvement of a parent in every stage of the learning process.

PLAYING WITH SAND AND WATER

Children usually find playing with water or sand very soothing and relaxing. Many of the basic play ideas and safety precautions* have already been mentioned on page 28. Below you will find more advanced games for slightly older children to try.

Water and sand play give children the opportunity to learn how natural materials behave and teach them about concepts such as quantity and capacity.

Physically, the play helps to develop their arm and hand muscles and improves their skill at pouring.

It is important to avoid the idea that getting wet or messy is naughty. Instead try to teach children to keep the mess within limits and make sure they help to clear up.

Baths and pools

Provide water and things to play with:

Make sure children cannot burn themselves on water from a hot tap. Weather permitting, the ideal place for water play is outdoors but wherever they play, expect spills. If you want to prevent clothes getting wet, provide wellingtons and plastic macs or aprons. You can buy plastic cuffs to keep sleeves dry.

Things to play with in water

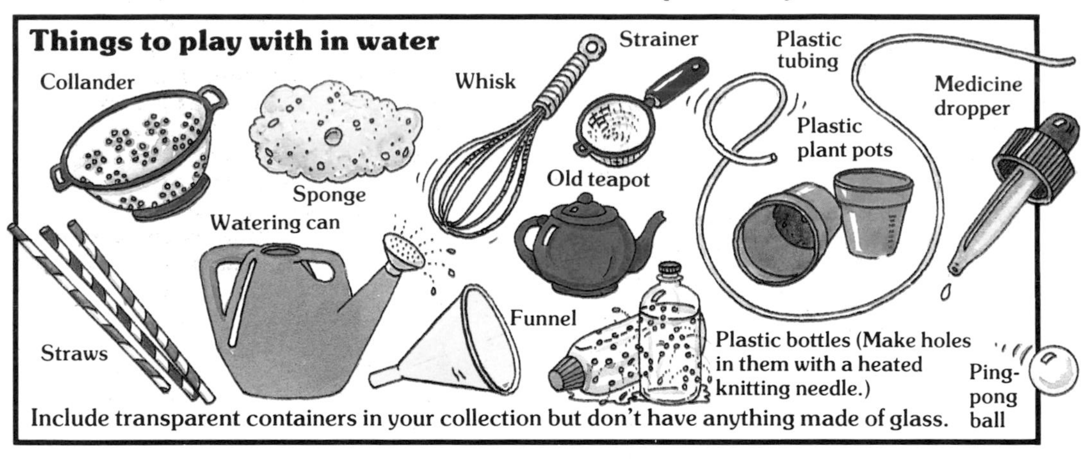

Include transparent containers in your collection but don't have anything made of glass.

Sand and sandpits

You do not have to buy or make a sandpit. Fill an old tyre with sand or just use a small amount in an old washing up bowl or baby bath.

Buy silver sand rather than builder's sand which stains clothes and skin.

Cover sand kept outdoors to stop it getting waterlogged and dirty – cats love using sand pits as dirt trays.

You can clean sand by rinsing it with water containing baby bottle sterilizer.

Make a rule that sand must never be thrown. If sand gets in someore's eyes, rinse them with plenty of cold water.

Things to play with in sand

Dry sand behaves rather like water, so many of the containers for water play are suitable. You could also try:

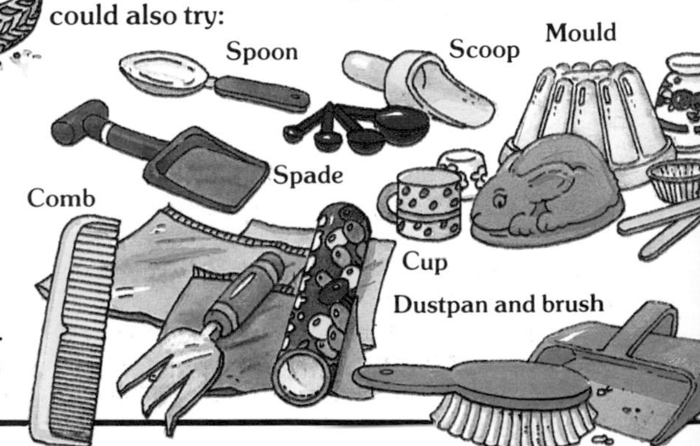

Remember that small children can drown in even small amounts of water and should never be left unsupervised.

Games with water

Floating and Sinking. Encourage experiments with different objects. Do they float or sink? How fast do they sink?

- Bottle tops (metal and plastic)
- Spoons (metal and plastic)
- Blocks of ice
- Wooden bricks
- Clothes-pegs
- Polystyrene
- Matches
- Raisins
- Marbles
- Buttons
- Corks
- Twigs
- Stones
- Leaves

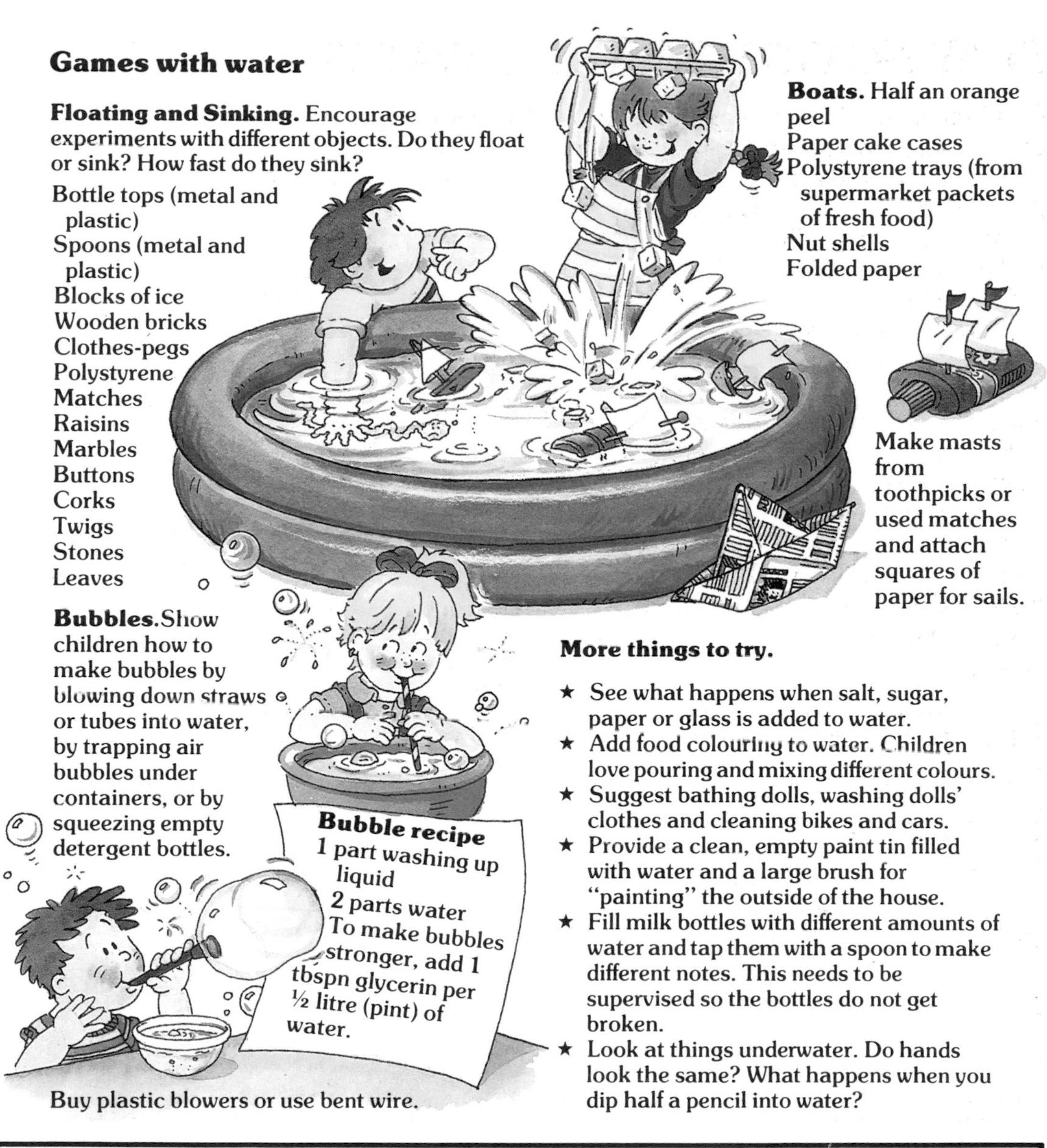

Boats. Half an orange peel
Paper cake cases
Polystyrene trays (from supermarket packets of fresh food)
Nut shells
Folded paper

Make masts from toothpicks or used matches and attach squares of paper for sails.

Bubbles. Show children how to make bubbles by blowing down straws or tubes into water, by trapping air bubbles under containers, or by squeezing empty detergent bottles.

Bubble recipe
1 part washing up liquid
2 parts water
To make bubbles stronger, add 1 tbspn glycerin per ½ litre (pint) of water.

Buy plastic blowers or use bent wire.

More things to try.

★ See what happens when salt, sugar, paper or glass is added to water.
★ Add food colouring to water. Children love pouring and mixing different colours.
★ Suggest bathing dolls, washing dolls' clothes and cleaning bikes and cars.
★ Provide a clean, empty paint tin filled with water and a large brush for "painting" the outside of the house.
★ Fill milk bottles with different amounts of water and tap them with a spoon to make different notes. This needs to be supervised so the bottles do not get broken.
★ Look at things underwater. Do hands look the same? What happens when you dip half a pencil into water?

Sand play ideas

Miniature worlds. Damp sand can be made into roads, bridges, tunnels, buildings. Add plastic or wooden vehicles, people or animals to make, say, a space station, town or farm.

Sand pictures. Use dry sand and a clean, flat surface. Pour the sand from a teapot or watering can so it makes a picture or pattern, or cover the surface with sand and let children draw in it with their fingers, a twig or a ruler.

Play cooking. Make exotic dishes using coloured sand, moulds, and scales to measure out the "ingredients". To find out how to colour sand see page 58

Weighing and measuring. A set of scales, especially the balance type, provide a lot of fun in a sandpit. Provide paper bags and cartons so they can play "shop" and spoon goods for sale into them.

DRESSING UP AND PRETENDING

There are several reasons why children enjoy dressing up and pretending. Dressing up can be fun just for its own sake, for the feel of the various materials with their different texture, weight, warmth and colour.

In dressing up to become another person or creature, a child can begin to imagine how it feels to be someone else. In their fantasy play, children are able to control situations in which they would normally be powerless and this helps to build confidence. They are also able to act out their fears and worries and so start to come to terms with them.

Talking out loud during the play is an important stage in learning to think clearly. Eventually children become able to follow their own thoughts without actually giving voice to them.
Fantasy play is equally common to both sexes. Parents sometimes worry if their sons dress up as fairies and princesses but this is quite normal.

On the practical side, dressing-up clothes should be simple to put on, should not be too long and have no dangerous cord round the neck. Children often regard dressing-up accessories, such as hats and bags, as more important than clothes.

Ideas for hats

Adapt hats by decorating them with things like ribbon, tissue paper, milk bottle tops, feathers and badges.

Try making simple hats out of card or thick paper. A basic cone shape is very adaptable.

Bands of different depths make different styles of hat.

Scarves or tea towels can make many different styles.

Things to collect

You can build up a good collection of dressing-up equipment from throw-outs. Ask friends and relatives, and look at jumble sales and in second-hand shops. Look for:

- ★ hats, bags, belts, gloves;
- ★ old jewellery, slides, bows, ribbons, spectacle frames, sunglasses;
- ★ scarves, stoles, shawls, aprons, petticoats, nightdresses;

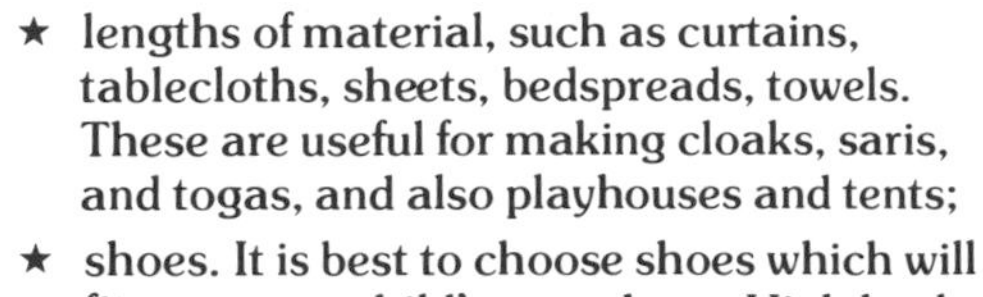

- ★ lengths of material, such as curtains, tablecloths, sheets, bedspreads, towels. These are useful for making cloaks, saris, and togas, and also playhouses and tents;
- ★ shoes. It is best to choose shoes which will fit over your child's own shoes. High heels are not very safe for under-fives.

Store everything together in, say, a large box or laundry basket but keep small items such as jewellery in a separate container. A mirror, preferably a full-length one, is fairly essential for dressing-up sessions.

Making jewellery

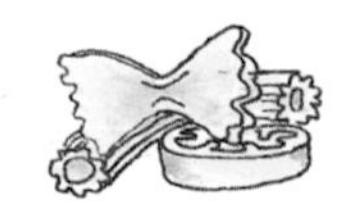

Pasta jewellery. Paint pieces of macaroni and other types of pasta which have a hole in them. When they are dry, thread them on shirring elastic to make necklaces, bracelets and ear-rings.

Card and paper jewellery. Make ear-rings, medallions, brooches and hair decorations like the ones shown below.

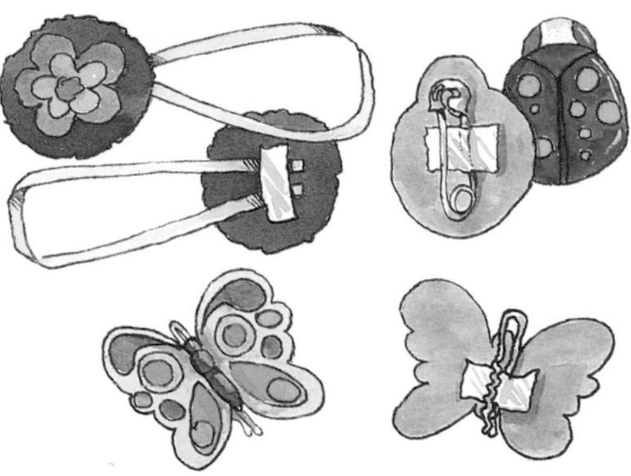

Playdough jewellery. Make pendants, brooches and ear-rings out of playdough baked in the oven. (See page 60 for the recipe.) When cool, paint with poster paints and, if you want a more professional finish, varnish.

Tape a safety pin to the back of brooches, as shown above.

Bits and pieces

- ★ False teeth (made from orange peel)
- ★ Spectacles (made from pipe cleaners)
- ★ Binoculars (toilet rolls)
- ★ Telescope (kitchen roll)
- ★ Various types of boots (decorated wellingtons)
- ★ Broken leg (wellington with strips of old sheet wrapped round it)
- ★ Soldier's hat (colander)
- ★ Chain mail (painted string vest)
- ★ Nurse's hat (shirt collar, starched if possible)

Making masks

Make a basic mask shape out of cardboard, for example a cereal packet or a paper plate. Cut two eye holes and a flap for the nose, and make a hole at either side.

Put rubber bands through the holes so they will fit over the ears, or just use ribbon, elastic or pipe cleaners to hold the mask on.

If your child dislikes the mask pressing against his face, try putting it on a stick instead.

Decorate with crayons or paints. You can also glue on hair (see below) and use glitter, sequins, gummed stars, bottle tops (for noses), split peas (for warts) and sticking plaster (for wounds).

For animal masks, stick on felt or fabric to represent fur and cut ears out of cardboard or stiff paper. Pipe cleaners make good whiskers; straws with cardboard circles on top good antennae.

Hair

Wool, cotton wool, raffia, string and wood-shavings all make good hair. Glue them to a mask or inside the rim of a hat. For curly hair, use wool unravelled from an old jumper or curl thin strips of paper round a pencil.

Wool glued to hat.

Curls on mask.

Old tights or stockings.

For beards and moustaches, glue the pretend hair to a cardboard or fabric base. Make holes in either side and fasten around the head in the same way as a mask.

Face paint

Discarded make-up or a packet of face paints provides a lot of entertainment. To clean them off afterwards, use cold cream and cotton wool followed by soap and water.

Play kits

Here are some ideas for pretend play situations.

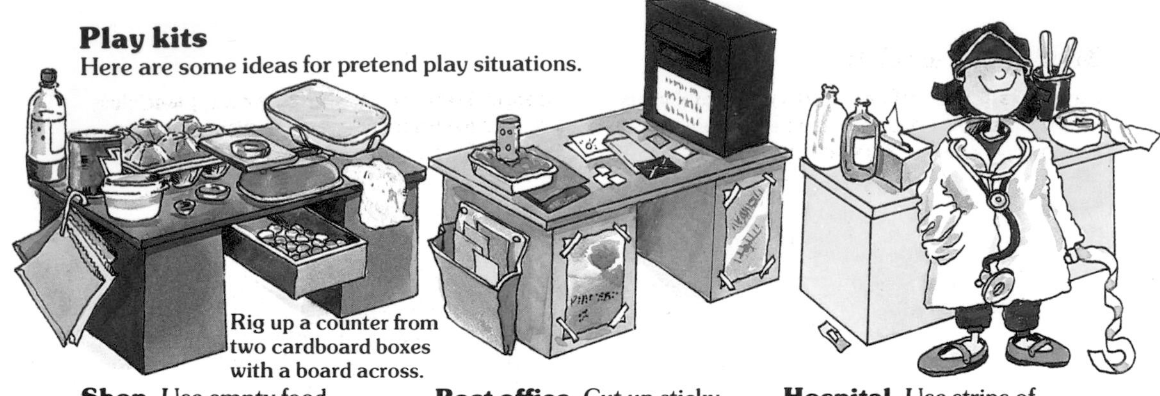

Rig up a counter from two cardboard boxes with a board across.

Shop. Use empty food packets and unopened tins, put the prices on sticky labels, have a toy cash register or use a shoe box as a till. Make money from milk bottle tops, cardboard and paper.

Post office. Cut up sticky labels for stamps. Save old stamp books, postcards and envelopes. Cut a slit in a box for posting. Have a stamp pad (kitchen paper soaked in paint) and a stamp (a cork).

Hospital. Use strips of material for bandages and masking tape for plasters. Save small plastic bottles. A small syringe (without the needle) and a toy stethoscope are both fairly cheap to buy.

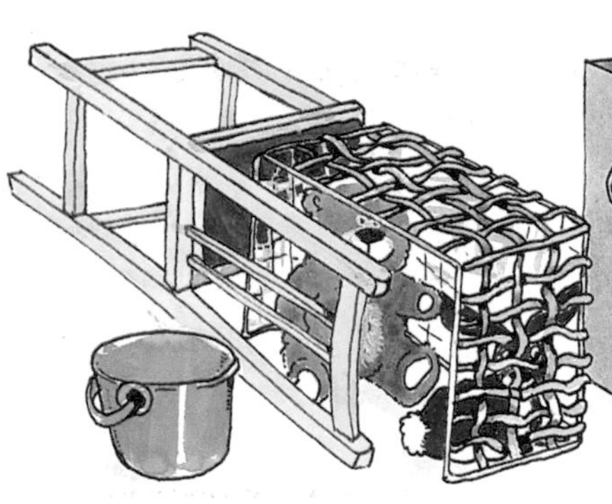

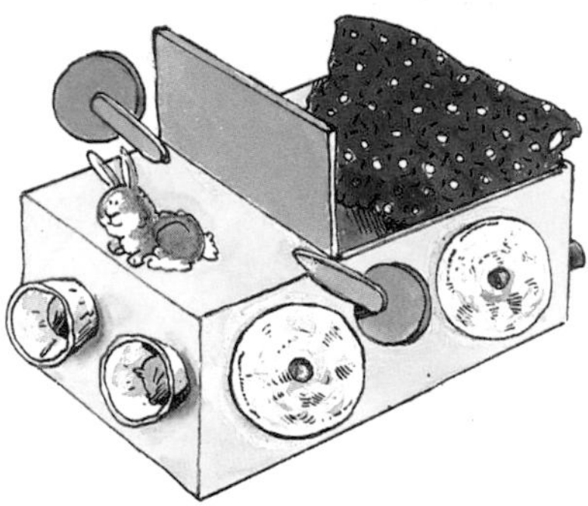

Zoo. Turn chairs with bars on to their sides and use fireguards to make cages. Put toy animals inside and provide a bucket so the keeper can feed them.

Aeroplane cockpit. Paint a large cardboard box or cover with coloured paper, then stick on a mass of knobs and dials made from bottle tops, jars and tubes.

Car. Add paper plate wheels and steering wheel to a big cardboard box. Paint a number plate on card. Use a sardine can key or any unused keys. Coloured tape makes good trim.

Playhouses and dens

There are many ways of making children their own private places to play in. Old curtains, sheets and blankets are useful, and so are giant cardboard boxes of the type new fridges and cookers are packed in. Whether the den represents a house, spaceship or cave, you will probably be asked to supply cooking and cleaning equipment, tables, seats and beds.

Miniature worlds

Cardboard boxes of assorted shapes and sizes can represent almost any type of building, such as a house, garage, farm or castle. Shoe boxes are especially useful. Pipe cleaners, plasticine and playdough are good for making people, animals, furniture and vehicles.

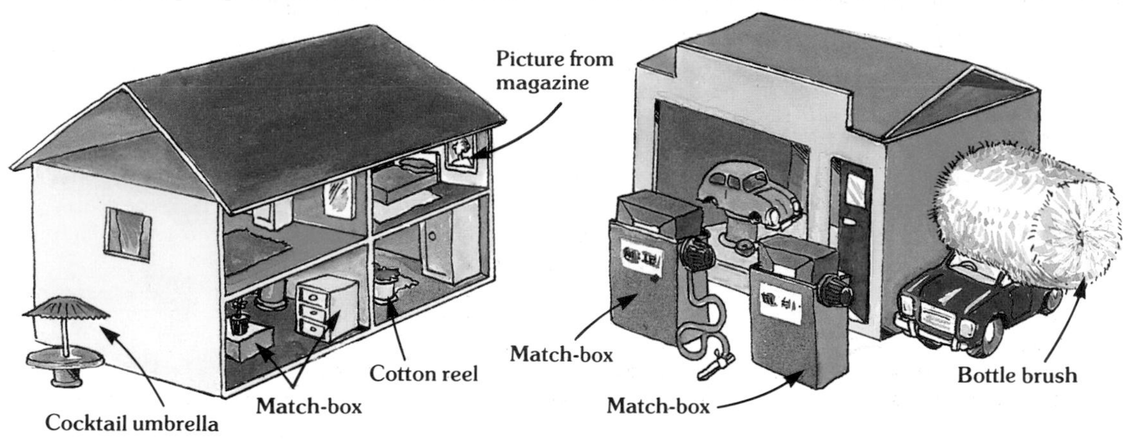

You can make a simple background for miniature buildings, people and objects by joining large sheets of paper together and drawing in roads, rivers, railways and fields with felt pen.

Puppets

Puppets are probably the easiest kind of "person" toy to make. Using them often encourages children to express hidden thoughts or feelings and to look at situations from a different viewpoint. (Specialists often use puppets with shy children and children with speech and other communication problems.)

Some children just play with puppets in the same way as they do with dolls. Some may want to put on a show. Some children dislike puppets and puppet shows so don't force them if they are not interested.

Paper bags. Draw a face on a bag, twist the corners for ears and hold in place on the child's hand with a rubber band round the wrist.

Socks. Stick or sew eyes on to an old sock. Show children how to put their hands inside and pull the toe of the sock in between their fingers and thumb to make a mouth.

Wooden spoons. Draw a face on a spoon and drape a scrap of material around the handle for a cloak.

Paper or felt. Make finger puppets by cutting out semi-circles, curling them into a tube shape and sticking them, so that they just fit over the fingers. Draw or stick on eyes, noses, ears and hats.

Match-boxes. Take the outside part of a match-box and glue on paper shapes for noses, eyes and ears. Use as a finger puppet.

Card. Cut an animal shape out of card. Cut two holes at the bottom to allow the fingers to poke through and act as legs.

IN THE KITCHEN

Children can get great satisfaction from making things and then eating them, and the kitchen provides them with endless opportunities for learning.

It gives them their first taste of science and the chance to learn about concepts such as quantity, shape and time. It can improve their counting and reading, increase their vocabulary, develop their manipulative skills and teach them how to concentrate and cooperate with another person.

An added bonus for parents is that cooking can sometimes help to cure fussy eaters.

Children need constant supervision when they are cooking and take a long time to do things, so if you are in a hurry don't let them join in.

There are several things in the kitchen that children might enjoy sorting into groups. Try giving them the cutlery tray, various root vegetables, different types of pasta or beans, or tins. If your scales are the balance type, you could give them an assortment of objects to balance and weigh. Or, if you can spare some cheap ingredients such as flour, oats, rice or pasta, let them do some play cooking with these. They can also learn a lot just by watching you cook.

Cooking tips and hints

Mixing or mashing. Put a damp cloth under the bowl or pan to stop it slipping.

Cutting. Start with a blunt knife and soft foods like bananas or bread, then cheese, before moving on to slightly sharper knives and harder fruits and vegetables.

Rolling out pastry. Explain how to dust the rolling pin and board with flour to stop the pastry sticking. A flour shaker is useful for this.

Measuring ingredients. Start by measuring in cupfuls and spoonfuls. Balance scales are much easier for children to understand than spring scales and make good playthings.

Greasing baking tins. Explain how to tilt the tin to catch the light so she can see if it has been greased thoroughly.

Sieving. Explain how to tap the side of the sieve rather than shaking it about. This stops the contents flying everywhere.

Following recipes. If your child is starting to recognize letters and numbers, you can write out your own simplified version of favourite recipes for him to follow.

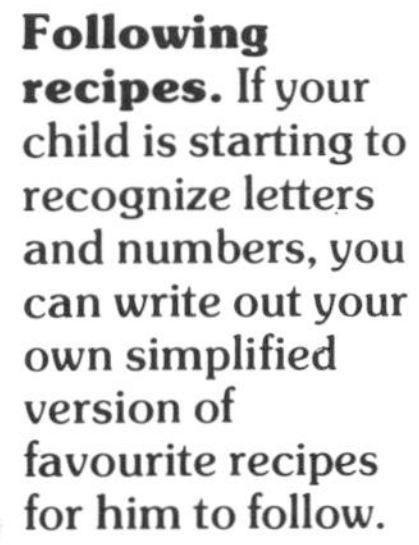

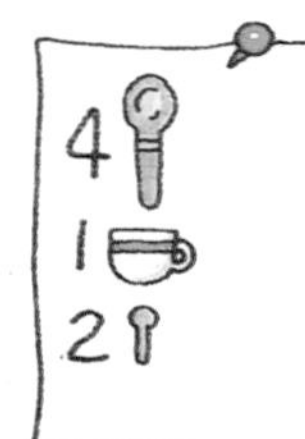

Decorating. Adding the final touches to a dish makes children feel they have had a big hand in making it even if they have done none of the preparation.

Safety and rules

Young children should always be supervised by an adult when they are cooking. For safety's sake it is worth making a few rules to follow in the kitchen.

- ★ Get together everything you will need before you start so that you do not have to leave your child unsupervised.
- ★ Teach children to wash their hands before cooking.
- ★ Teach them to be very careful when handling knives.
- ★ Teach them to ask before tasting anything.
- ★ If you spill something, clear it up immediately. One of you might slip on it.
- ★ If you use an electric mixer, teach children to keep their hands behind their back while it is on. Never put anything into the bowl while the mixer is going round.
- ★ Only do cook-in-the-oven recipes and don't let your child use the grill or rings. Turn saucepan handles so that they do not stick out over the edge of the cooker.

Making biscuits

Biscuits give plenty of scope for measuring, mixing, rolling out, shape-cutting and decorating. Below is a good basic biscuit recipe. Younger children will probably enjoy decorating them most.

Basic biscuit recipe
125g (4oz) soft margarine or butter
125g (4oz) sugar (white or brown)
250g (8oz) plain flour
1 egg
Pinch of salt

Beat the margarine and sugar together then beat the egg and add it to the mixture. Sift in the flour and salt, and mix to form a ball of dough. Roll out the dough and cut it into shapes. Put on a greased tray and bake in a moderate oven (approximately 190°C or gas mark 5) for about 15 minutes.

Decoration. Make a simple glacé icing from icing sugar and hot water (about 100g (3½oz) icing sugar to 1 tablespoon water) and perhaps a few drops of food colouring. Spread the icing on the biscuits with a knife or use a plastic icing syringe to make patterns, pictures or letters.

Decorate the biscuits with an assortment of the following: bought cake decorations, small sweets, dried fruit, chopped nuts, chopped glacé cherries and desiccated coconut. To avoid too much mess, put out the decorations in an empty egg box.

Experimenting with flavour. For biscuits with different flavours, try adding to the basic mixture some grated lemon or orange rind, melted or grated chocolate, mixed spice, cinnamon, ginger, dried fruit, chopped nuts, mixed peel or glacé cherries.

To make savoury biscuits, leave out the sugar and add some grated cheese or yeast spread. For sandwich biscuits, use a filling of jam, or icing sugar and butter creamed together.

Other things to try

Bread. Kneading is the part children enjoy. Lightly oil children's hands to stop the dough sticking to them. Divide the dough into small, manageable pieces.

Scones. Suggest making them into animal shapes or people and give them currant eyes.

Jam tarts. If you don't want to make pastry, buy some ready-made. Children enjoy rolling it out, cutting it into circles and putting them into a greased bun tin. Fill with jam, or mix golden syrup and breadcrumbs together to make treacle tarts.

Uncooked sweets. You can make peppermint creams, sugar mice or coconut creams from fondant icing (approximately 500g (1lb) of icing sugar to 1 egg white). Add a few drops of food colouring or flavouring as you choose.

Cake. Choose a basic all-in-one recipe. Children like tiny individual cakes in *petit-fours* cases. Decorate as for biscuits.

Drinks. If you have a blender you could try letting children make milk shakes, yoghurt drinks and fruit drinks.

Brandysnaps. The fun lies in trying to roll them round the handle of a spoon to make hollow pipes.

GROWING THINGS

Growing things makes children begin to realize where living things come from and what they need to survive. It also helps them to develop a sense of responsibility as they learn that plants will die if they do not look after them properly. It teaches them the difference between things grown just to look at and things grown to eat, and gives them an idea of the origins of various products.

Concentrate on quick-growing plants so your child does not lose interest before anything has happened and remember that home-grown plants make good presents.

Cress

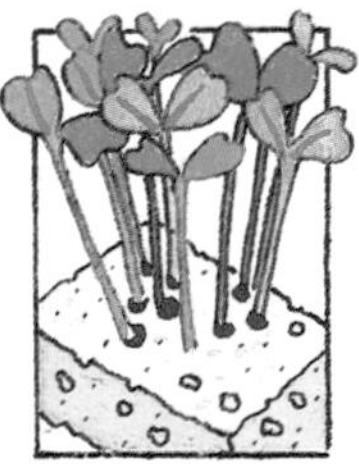

Cress is a favourite for children because it grows very quickly on almost any damp surface and you can eat it in sandwiches and salads.

Try growing it on cotton wool, several layers of kitchen roll or an old flannel or sponge.

Wet the growing surface, then pour off any excess water and sprinkle cress seeds thinly over it. Keep it warm and damp and within two or three days the cress should start to grow.

You can grow mustard mixed with cress but it tastes a bit strong for most children.

You can also grow grass seed, bird seed and even guinea-pig food in the same way. Make sure your child does not eat the results.

Cress words. Write your initials in seeds and watch them grow.

Cress clown. Draw a clown's face on an empty egg shell with felt pen. Fill the shell with damp cotton wool or kitchen roll and sprinkle cress seeds on top. Wait for the clown's hair to grow.

Miniature gardens

Provide an old meat tin or foil dish and collect damp earth, sand, moss, pebbles, twigs and flowers to arrange into a temporary garden. You could try growing some real grass seed. Include an old mirror for a pond or put water in a small, flat container and camouflage it. Add toy animals and people to the garden.

Other things to try

Broad beans or peas. Soak the beans or peas in water for 24 hours. Line a jam jar with damp kitchen roll and put about 2½cm (1in) of water in the bottom. Put the beans or peas between the paper and the glass, about half way down the jar. Put the jar in a light place and watch the roots and shoots forming.

Fruit pips. Soak orange, lemon or grapefruit pips in water for a day. Put them in a pot of soil or potting compost and cover them with ½cm (¼in) of the soil. Moisten. Put the pot in a polythene bag and loosely tie the top. Put in a warm place and keep the soil moist. Shoots should appear within a few days.

You can also grow peach, cherry or plum stones like this. Before potting, crack the stone without damaging the kernel.

LEARNING ABOUT ANIMALS

Children are naturally fascinated by animals and need to be given the opportunity to learn about them, perhaps through trips to places like zoos and farm parks. They can learn not to be afraid of animals but to have respect for them and, by extension, for all forms of life. Learning about animals also provides a good introduction to the subjects of birth, death and reproduction.

First pets

Though children can learn a lot from being pet owners, they cannot fulfil the responsibilities involved without a great deal of help. It may be better just to borrow small creatures from the wild for a short time. You can observe and care for them together, then let them go free.

Containers. Always provide as large a container as possible. Glass makes it easiest for you to observe the creatures. A small fish tank is ideal but a large pyrex dish or a glass bowl or jar will do. If a cover is necessary, punch air holes in it or use muslin.

Caterpillars. Look for these in hedgerows and gardens. Remove them gently with a paintbrush and take some of the plant you find them on. Don't keep more than three or four together and don't mix types. First they turn into chrysalises, then, after two or three weeks, into moths or butterflies. If they do not emerge after that time, spray them with a little water. Let the moths and butterflies go free.

Worms. Put alternate layers of sand and soil in your container. Then put in a few worms from the garden and some leaves for them to feed on. Keep the soil damp. Watch the worms working their way down through the layers and leaving their casts on the surface.

Other creatures. You could also try keeping snails, earwigs, woodlice or ladybirds. Always take some of the plant you find them on and put them in damp soil. Let them go free after a few days.

Feeding wild birds and animals

Birds. When you start feeding birds, they come to rely on you so continue feeding them right through the winter. Put the food high up out of the way of cats, somewhere where you will have a good view from a window. Different birds like:

Seeds (Collect from plants or buy bird seed.)
Bread
Bacon rind
Cheese
Dried fruit
Banana
Coconut
Peanuts (with or without shells but not salted)
Peanut butter
Suet

Make a bird pudding by mixing up scraps of these foods with melted fat and letting it set. Birds also need water to drink and bathe in.

Hedgehogs. You may be able to attract a hedgehog to your garden by leaving out a dish of milk.

Squirrels. Feed them on seeds and nuts. Take some with you if you are going for a walk amongst trees.

Thinking of buying a pet

Make sure you know exactly what is involved in the care and feeding of any animal, bird or fish you are thinking of keeping as a pet. Don't buy anything without considering all the disadvantages very carefully. It can be a good idea to start with something very simple like a goldfish.

COLLECTING THINGS

Children can learn a lot from making collections. An early enthusiasm for something could lead on to an interesting hobby later, and deciding how to keep, arrange or display things can provide useful opportunities for sorting and classifying. Many commercial toy companies trade shamelessly on the collector's instinct in children. Having their own special collections might make them slightly less susceptible to the pressures of the advertisers.

You may have to help by generating ideas, but don't pressurize a child to make a collection – some simply don't have the collector's instinct. Here are some things a child might get pleasure from collecting.

Tickets, e.g. bus and train tickets, tickets to the zoo, the cinema and other entertainments. Stick in scrapbooks with descriptions or drawings of outings.

Pebbles. Collect pretty shapes or colours. Also, encourage children to collect big, smooth pebbles and paint them or write and draw on them with felt pens.

Postcards. Collect as souvenirs and encourage friends and relations to send them whenever they are away from home.

Sweet wrappers, stamps, stickers.
Use them to make colourful posters.

Badges. These often come free for promotional purposes or with donations to charity. Collect or make them (see page 92) and display on board covered with felt.

Feathers. Having something to collect on walks makes them more interesting. This could well lead on to a real interest in birds.

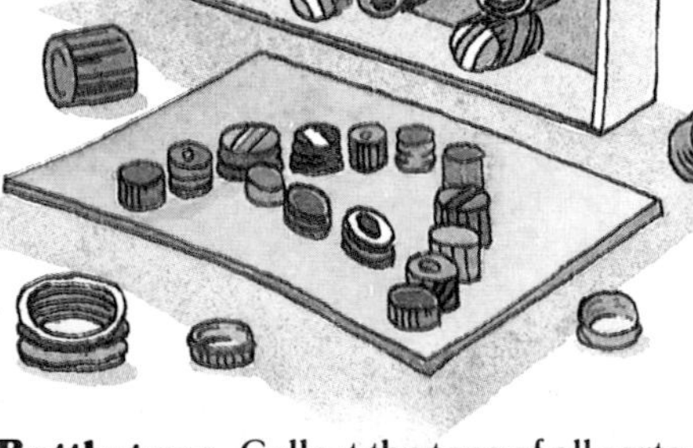

Bottle tops. Collect the tops of all sorts of different kinds of screw-top bottles, jars and tibes. Arrange in patterns or letter shapes.

Leaves. These are easier for small children to collect than flowers. Show them how to preserve leaves by pressing them between blotting paper under a pile of books.

GETTING EXERCISE

Exercise benefits almost everyone. It improves mood, appetite and quality of sleep and brings better general health. It is specially important for children – it develops their muscles, increases their strength and agility, and improves their co-ordination, balance and sense of timing. It also increases their understanding of the concepts of distance, height and space. Many children learn a lot about how to socialize by joining in physical activities.

The amount and type of exercise children get depends on individual circumstances: having a garden or using parks and playgrounds, having access to gym or movement and dance classes. It also depends on a child's inclinations; some children are naturally much more physically active than others.

Most children rarely attempt anything beyond their capabilities. It is best to interfere as little as possible when they are attempting some physical feat or you may actually increase the likelihood of an accident. Watch out, though, when they are playing with older children or are being goaded beyond their abilities.

Outdoor obstacle course

Below are some ideas to help you set up an obstacle course in the garden. You could also use them to set up an obstacle course for a tricycle, scooter or bicycle.

GOING SWIMMING

There are many good reasons for taking children swimming as early as possible: the younger they are the easier it is to learn to swim; children with some experience of swimming are safer when playing in or near water; swimming is excellent all-round exercise; it helps to develop breathing control and can be very relaxing; it is something the whole family can enjoy together and is often a good way to meet other children and parents.

Small children generally get on best if they are introduced to the water by one of their parents. If you yourself feel nervous of the water, try to go with another adult who is confident. Go to a shallow children's pool and if possible enrol in parent and child swimming classes.

Your general aim should be to get your child to enjoy himself in the water and to move freely backwards, forwards and sideways on his front and on his back, probably with buoyancy aids.

Keep each session short. Your child will learn more in short frequent visits than the occasional long one. Always get out before he begins to get cold, as small children's temperature regulating system is not yet very efficient.

Developing water confidence

Feeling happy and secure in the water is important if a child is to enjoy swimming. You can do quite a lot at home to develop his water confidence. Encourage him to get his face and head wet and to blow bubbles in the bath. Provide as many opportunities as possible for playing with water (see pages 74 and 75).

On your first visit to a swimming pool with your child it is a good idea to have a look around without actually swimming. This will give him a chance to see what will happen and get used to the strange atmosphere, noise and smell. Look at the changing rooms and lockers and talk about what you will do when you come next time. This will make you feel more confident as well, which in turn will affect your child's attitude.

Swimming classes

Parent and child swimming classes are held in increasing numbers nowadays and are an excellent idea, especially for parents who are not very confident in the water themselves. You can take part even if you cannot swim, although it is preferable to take lessons for adult beginners first.

At parent and child classes, there should be a qualified teacher to advise each parent how best to teach their child. The teacher will also organize games, sometimes with music to accompany them, may demonstrate exercises and provide a selection of toys for the children to play with, including some specialized ones for use in swimming pools.

Swimming pool facilities

Swimming pool facilities vary considerably. It can be well worth the effort of travelling a little further than is necessary to get to a pool that has particularly good facilities for young children. These include extra-warm water, an area of very shallow water or, better still, a completely separate pool for young children, non-slip floor surfaces and an easy way into the water. **(See page 36 for more details about facilities.)**

Things to do in the water

Hold your child close and bounce gently up and down in the water, so that you both get your shoulders wet.

Hold your child away from you and bounce up and down, then move forwards and backwards through the water.

Hold him under his chest and hips and encourage leg kicking and arm movement.

If child seems confident enough, let go.

Once he is used to the water on his body, get him used to splashes on his face and head.

Encourage him to put his face in the water and to blow bubbles.

Encourage her to put her head under the water and to open her eyes

Get her to move through the water by kicking and paddling. She may be fairly upright at first.

Encourage him to adopt a more horizontal position and then to push off from the side and glide.

When she is confident, encourage jumping in from the side.

Armbands and floats

Arm bands are really the best floating aid. They should be worn above the elbows. The double-chambered kind are the safest. You can gradually reduce the amount of air in them until they are no longer needed. Many children refuse to wear them at first, but if allowed just to play with them they usually consent in the end.

Polystyrene floats are useful for encouraging horizontal movement.

Rings tend to restrict movement and small children can fall out of them.

Water safety

Small children should always be closely supervised by an adult when near water, even if they can swim quite well. If they fall into cold water they can get into trouble very quickly.

You should always accompany them into the sea and insist that they stay in shallow water. Don't let them play on inflatable rafts or air beds and take any warning notices very seriously.

OUTINGS AND JOURNEYS

Children need to get out and about and benefit from experiencing as many different situations as possible. Remember that any walk or outing becomes more fun if it has a specific goal.

Children will feel more involved in an outing if you plan it with them beforehand and talk about it together afterwards. Use books and make pictures to follow up some of the things you have seen together.

Ideas for outings

The kind of outings you go on will obviously depend on your individual circumstances. The local paper and local library are good places to look for information about any special events in your area. Here are a few simple, general ideas for things to do.

Try a different form of transport from your usual one: for example, a short bus ride if you usually travel by car.

Go for a short train ride from your nearest station and back again.

Watch trains, especially at bridges or tunnels.

Watch boats on rivers or canals.

Watch aeroplanes. Most airports have a viewing platform.

Watch a building site, or roadworks.

Watch cars at a car wash.

Go on a picnic. You do not have to go far or take much with you.

Send yourselves a letter. Post it from your local box at collection time.

Get high up in, say, a department store or block of flats and spot landmarks.

Going shopping

Children enjoy shopping most if you let them get really involved. Let them look in the cupboards to see what is needed and help you make the shopping list. At the shops, they can find the goods on the shelves and hand the money to the cashier. When you can, make use of the things that specially appeal to children such as lifts, escalators and self-opening doors.

Shopping cards. Use pieces of card about the size of a postcard. On each card draw or stick a picture of something you frequently need to include on your shopping list. You could use distinctive bits of packaging on some of the cards. When you go shopping children can take the appropriate cards and help you find what you want by matching them to the goods on the shelves.

Games to play on journeys

Guessing games

★ How long is a minute starting from now?

★ How fast are we going?

★ Are we going to turn right or left next?

★ What colour will the next traffic light be at?

★ How long does it take to go a mile starting from now?

★ Who or what am I? Give clues, for example, "I am soft and furry and I purr"; "you use me to heat water".

Spotting games

★ I-Spy. Use colours instead of letters.

★ Choose a colour. The first to spot a car that colour chooses the next colour.

★ What will be the next animal we see?

★ Shout "rat-tat" if you see a post-box and "ring-ring" if you see a telephone box. First to spot either wins.

★ Cross your fingers if you see an ambulance or fire engine. Don't uncross them until you see a policeman or police car.

Other games

★ Keep quiet, or talk or sing for a minute.

★ One person asks questions. The others take it in turns to answer but must not say "yes", "no", "black" or "white".

★ One person says a word, for example "party". The next says a word she associates with the first, for example "jelly". And so on.

★ One person starts telling a story. The others take it in turns to add a section to it.

★ What's your name? Choose a letter of the alphabet and take it in turns to give a name starting with that letter. When you get stuck, you are out.

Ideas for long journeys

These take a little time to prepare.

Vehicle pictures. Cut out pictures of vehicles from magazines and put them in a large envelope or bag. Children take out one at a time and have to spot a vehicle to match it before moving on to the next one.

Lucky dip. Make a bag of surprises by wrapping up tiny presents individually. Ration them to last through the journey. Here are a few ideas for things to wrap:

Food: a few raisins, sweets or biscuits.

Toys: small pencils and notepads, a magic slate, puzzles and tricks, colouring pads.

For those who can read or recognize some letters: a secret message, name of a game to play, a song to sing.

Journey tapes. Make a tape and include stories, or one story in instalments, jokes, riddles, poems, songs and suggestions for games and things to spot.

PARTIES

It is not really practical to give children a proper party before they are three. Until then, it is better just to have a few friends to tea.

The key to a successful party is to plan ahead very carefully. This is vital. Keep the numbers small and the length of the party short. Two hours is long enough for three-year-olds. Put the starting and finishing time on the invitations.

Prepare more games than you think you will need. Keep each one short and stick to games with very simple rules that the children are likely to know already. Alternate energetic and quieter games and have a quiet one after tea and before the children go home.

Under-sevens cannot cope with too much competition, so adapt games to make them non-competitive or fix them so that everyone has a chance to win. If you have prizes, make sure that everyone wins one.

When the music stops

When you are playing musical games, try to make sure that the players cannot see exactly when the music is going to be turned on and off.

Musical bumps. Everyone jumps up and down in time to the music. Each time it stops, they all sit down. Pick out the last one to sit down, but don't make them sit out for the rest of the game. The winners can be the ones who have never been last.

Musical balloons. Have one fewer balloon than there are players. When the music stops each player has to grab a balloon. Spot the person without a balloon.

Hot potato. Everyone sits in a circle and passes round a potato. When the music stops, whoever has the potato must do a forfeit, such as run round the circle and sit down again.

Pass the parcel. Everyone sits in a circle and passes round a parcel with several layers of wrapping on it. When the music stops, the person holding the parcel starts unwrapping it. To sustain interest, try putting a little present between each layer of wrapping and fix the music stops so everyone gets a chance to do some unwrapping and find a present.

Other tips on avoiding disasters

★ Enlist other adults as helpers.

★ Make sure you have all the parents' telephone numbers.

★ Hide away any toys your child does not want to share.

★ Organize visits to the toilet for everyone after tea.

★ Plan the party with your child so that he knows what is going to happen and does not have unrealistic expectations.

Songs and stories

Action rhymes and songs go down well, if you have someone who is prepared to lead the singing. See pages 39-41, 71 and 72 to remind you of specific songs.

Similarly, you could have a story after tea if someone is willing to read or tell one.

Games for a limited space

Simon says. One person is Simon. He stands facing the others and shouts out instructions, such as "Simon says, 'touch your toes' ". Everyone has to obey. But if he leaves out the "Simon says", anyone who obeys the instruction is "out". As for musical bumps, it is best not to make the person sit out while you carry on until there is an overall winner.

Children find it quite hard to catch each other out, so limit the time everyone has as Simon and let adults have turns as well.

Squeak, piggy, squeak. Everyone sits on the floor except for one player, who is blindfolded. He tries to catch hold of the others. Each time he does, he says "Squeak, piggy, squeak" and the person has to squeak. If he guesses who it is, the squeaker is blindfolded.

Sneaky Peter. One person is blindfolded and sits on a chair with a teddy underneath it. The others try to sneak the teddy away without him catching hold of them. When someone is caught, he becomes It.

Duck, duck, goose. Everyone sits in a circle and one player is It. He walks round the outside of the circle, tapping each person lightly on the head and saying "Duck" with each tap. Finally, he taps and says "Goose". The goose jumps up and chases It round the outside of the circle. If It gets back to the empty space before Goose catches him, Goose becomes It.

Hunt the thimble/slipper/teddy/ sweets. You can either have one thing to hunt, which gets hidden again each time someone finds it, or have the same number of things hidden as there are children at the party. Hunting for little presents or sweets to take home makes a good ending to a party. You will have to stop some children from finding more than their fair share.

Sideshow activities

If you have a large party room and an extra adult to supervise, you can have these going on as the guests arrive or during the party for people who do not want to join in the main game.

Guessing games

- ★ How many sweets in the saucer?
- ★ How long is a minute?
- ★ What can you feel in the bag?
- ★ What food is it? (Blindfold tasting)

Throwing games

- ★ Throw the beanbag in the basket.
- ★ Throw the ping-pong balls in the jar.
- ★ Drop the clothes-pegs in the bottle.

Party themes

You could give a party with a special theme, which you can carry through the invitations, decorations and cake. Choose the theme with your child. You can rename all the games to fit the theme.

If you want the children to wear fancy dress, choose a theme for which outfits can be created quite simply – perhaps have a hat party or party with a colour theme.

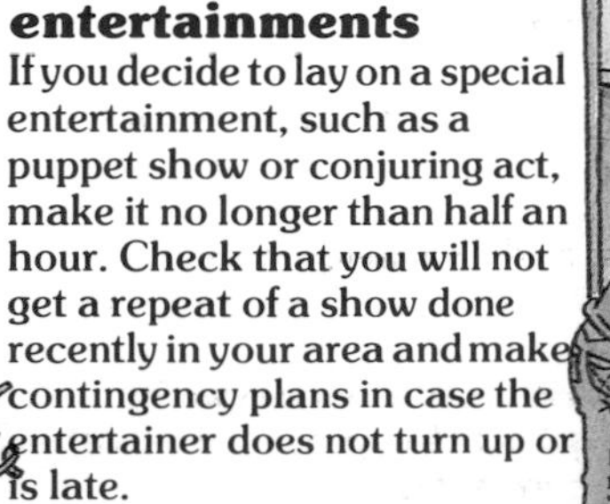

Special entertainments

If you decide to lay on a special entertainment, such as a puppet show or conjuring act, make it no longer than half an hour. Check that you will not get a repeat of a show done recently in your area and make contingency plans in case the entertainer does not turn up or is late.

Wet afternoons and other difficult times

Many of the other chapters in this book will give you ideas for the times when you cannot take children out and they are feeling fed up and need to get involved in some absorbing activity.

You may like to keep a box of toys for use only on these occasions, or have a secret selection of colouring books and puzzle books tucked away. Story tapes can also come in handy, especially for children who are not feeling well. The selection of ideas on these two pages may also be useful.

Catching cone

Make a cone and attach a ping-pong ball, or some other light object to it. Try to catch the ball in the cone.

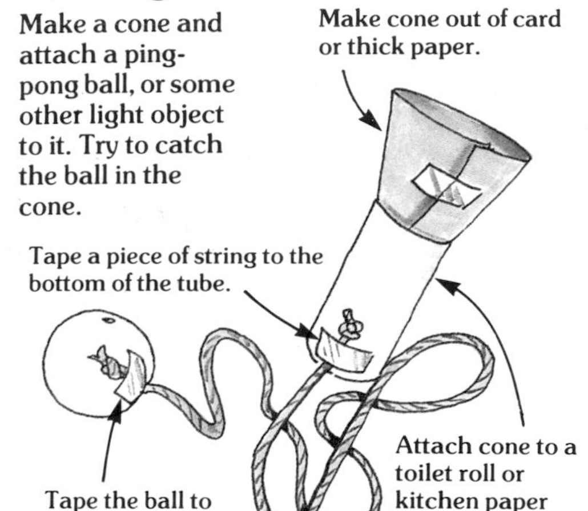

Sewing cards

Use old Christmas or birthday cards, or draw very simple pictures on pieces of card. Make holes along the outline of the objects in the pictures. Thread a large, blunt needle with wool or embroidery silk, so that your child can sew round the outlines. Instead of needle and thread you could use long shoelaces or string, stiffened at the end with sellotape.

Skittles

Use empty plastic bottles as your skittles and a fairly large ball. Start by standing quite close. A narrow hallway is an ideal place to play. If you do not have any plastic bottles you could use yoghurt pots or plastic cups stuffed with newspaper. Instead of a ball, try rolling a potato.

Fun with balloons

Blow up balloons, then let them go to see whose goes the furthest. Use felt pens to make them look like insects, monsters or members of the family.

Attach a piece of string between two chairs and use bats or hands to have a game of balloon tennis.

Badges

Help children to cut out badge shapes from pieces of card. Squares, oblongs and triangles are easier to cut than circles. Decorate with felt pens and coloured sticky paper. Attach safety pins to the back with sticky tape or sticking plaster.

Torch tag

Each person has a torch and directs its beam on to the ceiling in a darkened room. One of the spots of light is "It" and has to try and catch the others. If you have any tissue paper or coloured cellophane, you could put a different colour over each torch, using rubber bands to hold them in place. When one light catches another the colours mix.

Magnets

It is worth buying a large horseshoe magnet for children to experiment with. They can have a lot of fun just testing to see what is magnetic and what is not. If you have some paper clips, you could make paper characters to slot into them, as shown on the right. Put the characters on a piece of flat cardboard propped up on two piles of books, and use the magnet underneath the cardboard to move them around. You could make up a story and move each character as it is mentioned.

Paper darts

Follow the steps shown here to make paper darts. See who can throw their dart furthest or make one land on the table. It can take a bit of practice to learn how to throw a dart.

1
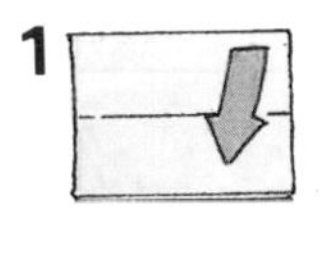
3
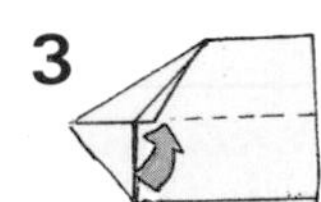
5
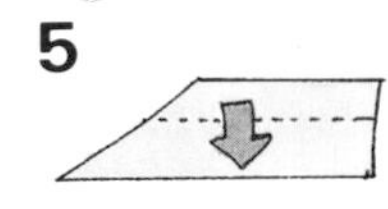
2
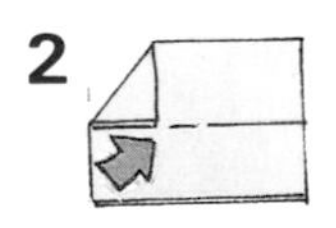
4
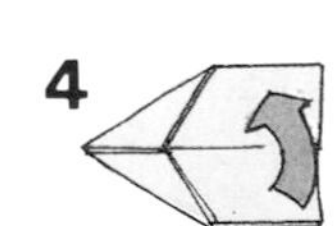
6
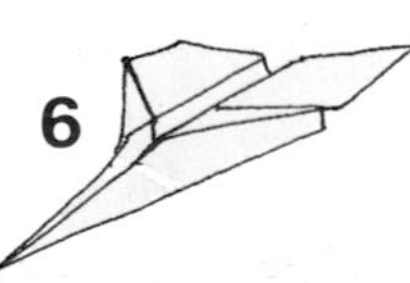

Stunts

Get children to try doing these things:

★ Rub stomach in a circle with one hand, while patting head with the other.

★ Make a "3" in the air with one hand, while making an "0" in the air with the other.

★ Stand facing someone and copy every movement that they make, as though they were a mirror.

★ Sing one nursery rhyme, such as "Baa, baa, black sheep", while someone else sings another one, such as "Ring a ring o'roses".

Wet afternoon box

Here is a selection of things you might find it useful to keep in a special box which you keep for use when you have run out of other ideas and the situation looks desperate:

Soft ball (felt or foam for use indoors)
Ping-pong balls
Torches and spare batteries
Horseshoe magnet
Balloons
Sticky paper shapes
Old Christmas and birthday cards
Magnifying glass (Look at all sorts of things – hands, pictures, writing, food, carpets, sponges.)

THE STUDY OF PLAY

A hundred years ago few people would have looked upon play as having an important part in a child's development. Playing was something children did when they had nothing more important to do. Today there is a growing interest in the relationship between play and human development. Many universities now have departments or units devoted to this subject and most of the research is concentrated on the pre-school years.

The development of the study of play

Interest in play developed alongside the realisation that the conditions and experiences of childhood had an important effect upon later life. The work of philosophers, such as Rousseau, and naturalists, such as Darwin, challenged and eventually changed the view that children were little adults developing according to some preordained plan. This changed view of childhood naturally led on to an interest in play.

Early views of play saw it as a principally physical activity – a way of releasing surplus energy no longer required purely for survival. As the field of psychology developed, so did more sophisticated views of play and childhood. Play was seen to involve intellectual and emotional activity as well as physical.

Theories about play

Many different theories about play have been developed over the years, but the main areas of approach can be seen in the work of three great psychologists: Sigmund Freud, Jean Piaget and Jerome Bruner.

Freud was concerned with the function of play in emotional development. His work focussed on fantasy play and, in particular, on the link between play and a person's unconscious self. He claimed that the unconscious finds expression through play, and he developed two explanations for how this might operate. Firstly, children play in order to gain control of unpleasant feelings; and secondly children play to fulfil unconscious desires. Although much of Freud's work is now being questioned, it is still generally accepted that play is a way in which children can express their feelings and work through emotional disturbances.

Freud's approach contrasts strongly with that of the Swiss psychologist, Jean Piaget, whose theories of how the intellect develops underpin much modern educational practice. Broadly speaking, he saw play as a means of practising what has been learnt, of perfecting newly-acquired skills, and of demonstrating that new skills had been learnt and perfected.

Both Freud and Piaget believed that children outgrew play once their emotional and intellectual skills had reached a certain point of development and this aspect of their work is strongly contested today. Piaget's work is also criticised by more modern theorists for denying play a more active role in the way children learn. Bruner, for example, sees play as a means of actively acquiring information, constructing new ideas and developing skills.

The bulk of investigation into play is still undertaken by psychologists interested in child development.

The importance of play

Despite the growing interest in and study of the subject, there is still no single definition of play that is totally satisfactory. However, there is now little doubt about the importance of its contribution to nearly all aspects of development. Current research is exploring the conditions which are best for maximising the potential benefit of play to children's development and adult involvement is now generally seen as an important enhancing factor to the quality of children's play. The main role of the adult is to provide enough stimulating opportunities for different types of play.

INDEX

First published in 1987 by Usborne Publishing Ltd, 20 Garrick Street, London WC2 9BJ, England.

 Printed in Belgium.